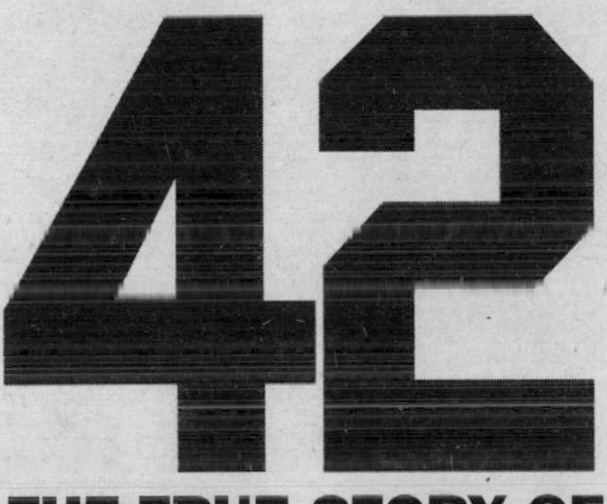

THE TRUE STORY OF JACKIE ROBINSON

THE TRUE STORY OF JACKIE ROBINSON

Adapted by
Aaron Rosenberg

Based upon the screenplay written by
Brian Helgeland

Scholastic Inc.

ISBN 978-0-545-53753-7

Published by Scholastic Inc.

12 11 10 9 8 7 6 5 4 3 2 1 13 14 15 16 17 18/0

Printed in the U.S.A. 40
First printing, March 2013

CHAPTER 1

hree men sat in the office on Montague Street. The blinds were closed, and what little light leaked in caught the dust motes in the air, making them sparkle like flecks of gold. A fish tank bubbled against one wall, the goldfish within darting merrily this way and that. On the wall behind the desk hung two framed photos, one of Abraham Lincoln and the other of Brooklyn Dodgers coach Leo Durocher. A massive chalkboard occupied a third wall, its dark surface covered with names. None of the men so much as glanced at it. Branch Rickey, the man behind the desk and the Dodgers' general manager, was not pleased.

"Gentlemen," Rickey announced, "I have a plan." He looked surprisingly nervous but determined, his shaggy eyebrows low over his round spectacles. "As of now, only the board of directors and my family know."

The two men in front of him exchanged a look. Clyde Sukeforth was a talent scout and a member of the Dodgers' coaching staff. Harold Parrott had been a sportswriter before becoming the Dodgers' traveling secretary a few years earlier. As the organization's general manager, Rickey was their boss, and both of them respected him a great deal.

"A plan's always good, Mr. Rickey," Sukeforth offered. "And you always got one." That was true. Rickey had proven himself as the manager of the Cardinals, leading them to a World Series title before replacing Larry McPhail as the head of the Dodgers in 1943. That was two years ago, and he had done well by the team so far.

But Rickey sighed and shook his head. "My wife says I'm too old," he confessed. "That my health isn't up to it. My son says that everyone in baseball will be against me. But I'm going to do it."

"Do what, Mr. Rickey?" Sukeforth asked.

Rickey smiled. "I'm going to bring a Negro ballplayer to the Brooklyn Dodgers."

His two employees looked startled, and Parrott finally opened his mouth. "With all due respect, sir," he said, "have you lost your mind? Imagine the abuse you'll take from the newspapers alone. Never mind how it'll play on Flatbush. Please, Mr. Rickey."

Sukeforth was shaking his head as well, and it was toward him that Rickey directed his reply. "There's no law against it, Clyde."

"There's a code," Sukeforth shot back. "Break a law and get away with it, some people think you're smart. Break an unwritten law, though, you'll be an outcast."

But Rickey was clearly determined. "So be it," he declared, holding his head high. "New York is full of Negro baseball fans; every dollar is green. I don't know who he is, or where he is, but he's coming."

Parrott looked mutely at Sukeforth, but the scout only shrugged. It was obvious they weren't going to change the boss's mind.

Meanwhile, in Birmingham, Alabama, a spirited baseball game was taking place. It was April 8. The Birmingham Barons and the Kansas City Monarchs had been at each other's throats all night. Right now, however, it was one particular Monarch who was getting under the Barons' skin.

"Where'd you learn to move like that, runner?" the Barons' catcher shouted at the player currently on first, who was

restlessly hopping from foot to foot. "At dime-a-dance night? Stay quiet!"

The runner just laughed—and the moment the first pitch left the mound, he took off. John Scott, the Monarch currently at bat, swung and missed, and the catcher shot up, firing the ball to second, but too late. The runner slid into second base safely. He hopped up to his feet with one foot solidly on the bag and dusted himself off.

"Is that the best you got?" he taunted the catcher. "Huh? I'm going to steal nine, ten bases today! You better start counting!"

The catcher frowned and rose from his crouch. He was a big man, big enough to tower over Scott. "Where's your short-stop from?" he asked the batter, his Alabama accent dragging at the words.

"California," Scott answered, eyeing him warily.

"He's got a mouth on him." The catcher dropped back into position and signaled the pitcher. Scott breathed a sigh of relief and raised his bat—but the second the ball flew, so did the runner. Again. And again the catcher tried to catch him out, but his throw reached third base after the man had.

"Safe!" the umpire declared.

"You got a rag arm, catcher!" the runner shouted, laughing.

"Yeah?" the catcher replied. "Steal home! You'll find out what kind of arm I got!"

The runner grinned. "Okay, I'm coming!"

Scott chuckled, and the catcher glared at him. "California, huh? Well, California here he goes, if he comes down here."

Play resumed, and the pitcher hurled a fastball over the plate. Again the runner took off, this time heading home like a bullet. Scott swung and missed, and just as the catcher got his glove on the ball, the runner slid in. The catcher slammed both hands, glove, ball, and all, right into the runner's face!

Wham!

The runner lay there for a second, stunned. Finally, he rose to his feet, shaking his head. The first thing he did was look at the umpire.

"What was I?" he asked, his voice as wobbly as his legs.

The umpire responded by passing one hand over the other. Safe! The runner had scored!

Triumphant, Jack Roosevelt Robinson glared at the catcher smugly. But as he turned to head for the dugout, the catcher shoved him in the back. Jackie turned and shoved back. Then the two of them were on the ground, pushing and punching, the umpire's whistle going unnoticed in the heat of battle.

It was just another night in the Negro Leagues, and just another game for Jackie. A few hits, a few stolen bases, a few fights—all par for the course.

It was mid-August, and Rickey and Sukeforth sat in Rickey's office. Stacks of files covered the desk, each one with a black ballplayer's picture clipped to the front.

"What about this one?" Sukeforth asked. He held up a file. "Josh Gibson. Oh, boy, can he hit." But Rickey shook his head. "All right. Roy Campanella?"

"A heck of a player," Rickey agreed, "but too sweet—they'll eat him alive."

Sukeforth nodded. Whoever they picked would surely need a thick skin to put up with all the abuse he was likely to get. He selected another folder. "Satchel Paige, then." Paige played for the Monarchs and was already a legend. There was nobody better.

But again Rickey shook his head. "Too old," he said. "We need a man with a future, not a past." Which was true enough. Paige was already thirty-nine, and in baseball a lot of players had retired by that age.

The door opened, and Parrott entered, carrying an armful of files himself. He set them on the desk, but they began to slide off immediately, spilling to the floor. Parrott tried to stop them, but it was hopeless. His expression said he thought that was true of this whole enterprise.

But Rickey was undeterred. One of the fallen files caught his eye and he scooped it up. "Here," he said. "Jack Roosevelt Robinson." He flipped through the file. "A four-sport college man, out of UCLA. That means he's played with white boys." He kept reading, liking what he saw. "Twenty-six years old, now with the Kansas City Monarchs. Batting over three fifty even as we speak. Three fifty! Says here he's a Methodist. Says he was a commissioned army officer!"

This time it was Sukeforth who shook his head. "He was court-martialed," he told Rickey. "A troublemaker. He argues with umpires. Has a quick temper."

"Oh." Rickey sighed and tossed the file back onto the desk. A quick temper was exactly what they didn't need.

"How about Larry Doby?" Sukeforth offered. "Newark Eagles. Heck of a player."

"Too young. Inexperienced." Rickey glanced toward the window, the dejection clear in his voice, and Parrott and Sukeforth both held their breaths. Could this be the end of this crazy idea? But then their boss straightened. "Hold on," he demanded. "What exactly was Robinson court-martialed for?"

"Something about refusing to sit in the back of a bus," Sukeforth answered. He picked up the file and checked it. "Yeah, it was in Fort Hood, Texas. The driver asked him to move back. The MPs had to take him off."

Rickey nodded, his fire back. "There you are. He resents segregation. If he were white, we'd call it spirit!" Sukeforth shrugged. He didn't look convinced. Neither did Parrott. But their boss was. "Robinson's a Methodist," Rickey declared. "I'm a Methodist. God's a Methodist. We can't go wrong. Find him. Bring him here." Without another word, he stood and stepped away from the desk, taking Jackie Robinson's file and leaving all the others behind. Sukeforth and Parrot could see that Rickey's mind was made up.

A few days later, a beat-up old bus with a banner that read "KC Monarchs" pulled into a service station on the road from Birmingham to Chicago. An attendant sauntered out of the station to greet the driver as he stepped off the bus, but barely spared a glance for the black ballplayers as they followed, stretching after the long ride.

"Fill her up?" the attendant asked the driver. The driver nodded, and the attendant started unscrewing the caps on the bus's two fifty-gallon tanks.

Jackie had just stepped down, legs aching like the rest—but something else was aching worse. Glancing around, he spotted the bathroom off to the side of the station and headed toward it.

"Hey!" the attendant shouted when he noticed. "Where you going, boy?"

Jackie stopped and glanced back. "I'm going to the toilet."

The attendant shook his head. "C'mon, boy. You know you can't go in there." He gestured at the door, and the sign on it that read "White Men Only."

Jackie frowned fiercely. Then he turned and stomped back toward the attendant. "Take that hose out of the tank," he demanded, his voice a low growl.

"Huh?" The attendant just stared at him, unsure how to respond.

"Robinson—" the driver started, but Jackie cut him off.

"Take it out," he insisted. "We'll get our ninety-nine gallons of gas someplace else."

The attendant blinked. Then he glanced past Jackie, out toward the highway. It was deserted and had been all day. Finally, he sighed. "Okay, use it. But don't stay in there too long."

Jackie nodded curtly and resumed his march toward the restroom. Behind him, the other players looked on, stunned. None of them would have dared to try that.

Inside the tiny restroom, Jackie used the facilities, flushed, washed, and then splashed water on his face. He heard a bell ding outside as he patted his face dry with a paper towel—another

customer had arrived. Good thing that hadn't happened a few minutes earlier!

Stepping back outside, he saw a snazzy car parked beside the bus. Its driver was busy talking with several of the Monarchs. They all looked up as Jackie approached.

"Are you Jackie Robinson?" Clyde Sukeforth asked. When Robinson nodded, he smiled and gestured toward the passenger seat. "Great, get in. I've got somebody wants to meet you, back in Brooklyn."

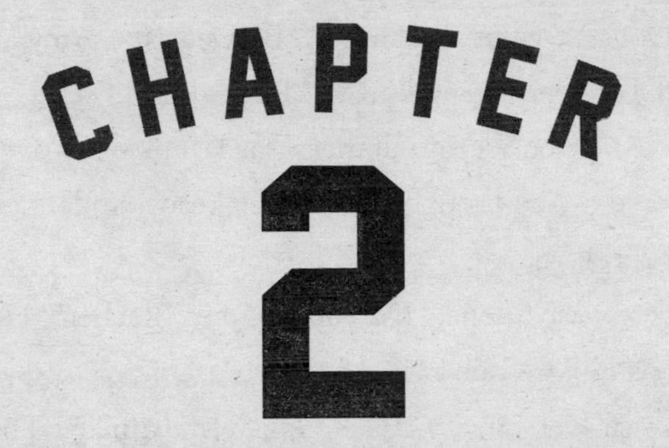

CHAPTER 2

Jackie strained to focus in the gloom of Rickey's office. The blinds were closed again. Rickey sat behind the desk, studying him closely, the dim light gleaming off his glasses. Sukeforth was seated against the wall, well out of the way.

"Do you have a girl?" Rickey demanded suddenly.

Jackie stared at him. "Excuse me?"

"A man needs a family relying on him," Rickey explained. "It ensures he'll behave responsibly. Do you have a girl?"

"I think so," Jackie answered.

Rickey's thick brows drew together. "You *think* so?"

Jackie glanced at Sukeforth, who just smiled. Then he turned back to Rickey. "I don't make much money," he admitted to the Dodgers' general manager. "Between the army and now baseball, I've been away a lot. And Rae—Rachel—she wants to finish school. Considering all that, I say I think so." Nonetheless, he warmed at the thought of her, her ready smile, her warm laugh, her bright eyes.

Rickey wasn't done. "Do you love her? Rachel?" He noted Jackie's pause. "Or don't you know?"

"Yes, sir, very much," Jackie answered finally. The delay hadn't been because he didn't know his own heart. He just wasn't sure where this conversation was going, which was why Rickey's next words really floored him:

"Marry her." He stood and walked over to the window. Jackie glanced questioningly at Sukeforth, who gestured for him to stay put and keep listening.

"Baseball's a hard life," Rickey continued. "A man needs a good woman by his side. You don't want the only person waiting for you at home to be a catcher." Sukeforth chuckled as Rickey fingered open a slat on the blind and peered out, almost as if he were bored with this conversation.

Enough of this nonsense, Jackie decided. *Time to get down to brass tacks.* "Coach Sukeforth here said you were starting a new Negro League," he declared. "That doesn't make sense to me."

"It doesn't, huh? Are you calling us liars, Jack?" Rickey hadn't turned around.

"What's this about, Mr. Rickey?" Jackie asked. He was starting to wonder if the long car ride had just been a waste of time.

"About?" Rickey answered. "This is about baseball." He opened the shade then, and sunlight flooded into the room. The beams illuminated the chalkboard on the far wall, and Rickey followed them over, stopping beside a list of players.

"I see you starting in the spring with our affiliate in Montreal," he announced, studying the board. "If you make it there, we'll try you down here with the Dodgers. The white Brooklyn Dodgers."

Jackie just stared at him. A black man joining a white team—was that even possible? He glanced at Sukeforth, who nodded. He couldn't tell if the talent scout liked the idea or not.

"I'll pay you six hundred a month," Rickey continued, "and a thirty-five-hundred-dollar bonus when you sign the contract. Is that agreeable?"

Jackie gulped. "Yes, sir," he managed. "That's fine." Fine? That was an astounding amount of money, especially for a young black man. Could this really be happening?

"There is one condition," Rickey added. "I have a pile of scouting reports on you. I know you can hit behind the runner, that you can read a pitch. The question is, can you control your temper?"

"My temper?"

Suddenly, Rickey turned from the board. "Yes, your temper!" he snapped. "Are you deaf?" Jackie glared at him, balling his fists, but didn't move another muscle. "He looks proud," Rickey told Sukeforth. "Willful."

"He'll need to be," the scout pointed out, and Jackie thought he heard grudging admiration in the man's voice.

Rickey turned back to Jackie. "I want to win!" he announced. "I want ballplayers who can win! Are you one of them?"

That, at least, Jackie could answer. "Yes."

"A black man in white baseball. Imagine the reaction. The vitriol." Rickey took a step forward and got right in Jackie's face. "The Dodgers check into a hotel. A good, decent hotel. You're worn out from the road and some clerk won't give you the pen to sign in." He affected a Southern drawl. "'We got no room, boy, not even down in the coal bin where you belong.'" Jackie was scowling now, banging his hands on the arms of the chair as Rickey continued. "The team stops at a restaurant. The waiter won't take your order." His voice shifted again. "'Didn't you see the sign on the door? No animals allowed.' What are you going to do then?" he demanded. "Fight him? Ruin all my plans? Answer me!"

A cold, hard look settled on Jackie's face. "Do you want a ballplayer who doesn't have the guts to fight back?" he asked, barely able to force the words out through his anger. "Is that what you want?"

"I want one who has the guts *not* to fight back!" Rickey shot back. "There are people who won't like this. They will do anything to get you to react. If you echo a curse with a curse, they'll only hear yours. Follow a blow with a blow, and they'll say a Negro lost his temper, that the Negro does not belong. Your enemy will be out in force, but you cannot meet him on his own low ground. We win with hitting, running, and fielding—nothing else. We win if the world is convinced of two things: that you are a fine gentleman and a great ballplayer. Like our Savior, you must have the guts to turn the other cheek."

The two of them stared at each other, the fiery general manager and the equally volatile young player.

"Can you do it?" Rickey asked. His voice had gone soft, all the fire burned out of him. For now.

Jackie considered the question seriously. He knew there would be no turning back. That he wasn't sure he could deal with the scrutiny and harassment Rickey was describing. But he also knew he had to try.

"Mr. Rickey," he said finally, meeting the other man's eyes, "you give me a uniform, you give me a number on my back, and I'll give you the guts."

Rickey smiled, nodded, and clapped a hand on Jackie's shoulder. Then he looked over at Sukeforth, who gave him a thumbs-up. They had their player.

An hour later, a phone rang in the Los Angeles home of the Isum family. Twenty-three-year-old Rachel crossed the room gracefully and answered it.

"Hello?"

"Rae?" It was Jackie. "Rae, I'm in Brooklyn." She could hear the sound of people bustling about in the background.

"Brooklyn?" she asked. "For what?"

"I don't want to say on the phone," he answered. "In fact, I'm not supposed to tell anyone." She could hear his excitement, though.

"Jack?"

"I'm here, Rae."

"What's going on? You're supposed to be playing in Chicago!"

He laughed at that, his happy laugh, not his bitter one. "We've been tested, you and me," he told her. "Our loyalty, our faith. We've done everything the right way. Me trying to make money. You finishing school. Separated by the war, now by baseball. We don't owe the world a thing. Only each other."

She wasn't following him. "Jack, what are you talking about? What happened?"

He laughed again, and it was sheer joy. "The Brooklyn

Dodgers just signed me to play ball up in Montreal," he answered. "It might lead to bigger things. To something wonderful."

"That's wonderful," she agreed. "But what does it mean? For you and me?"

His voice turned serious. "Rae, will you marry me?"

She didn't even have to think about it. "Absolutely. When?"

"Now."

This time she laughed. "Jack, I don't think we can get married in a phone booth."

Two nights later, Jackie rounded a corner in the Clark Hotel in Los Angeles. He looked dashing in his tux, though the bow tie was now undone. Rachel was walking by his side, her hand clasped in his, radiant in her wedding gown.

"Did my mom look happy?" she asked as they reached the hotel room door and Jackie pulled out a key to unlock it.

"Yes," he answered absently, concentrating on the key and the lock.

"Did my gram look happy?" She took a step back as he unlocked the door. Everything was moving so fast!

He smiled. "Everyone looked happy. I've never seen so many people looking happy."

"Did Jack Robinson look happy?" she asked softly, the full

weight of what they'd done looming over her suddenly. "What if I can't make you happy?"

"Too late," he assured her as he turned and took her hands. "You already do. It's you and me, Rae."

She smiled, basking in the love she felt flowing from him. "Until the wheels fall off."

Wendell Smith sat before Rickey's desk, studying the Dodgers manager in the dim light. He blinked behind his glasses.

"Who's the best shortstop you ever saw?" Rickey was asking him.

"Rabbit Tavener," Smith replied.

That got a snort. "Rabbit Tavener? And you call yourself a sportswriter?" Smith covered baseball for the *Pittsburgh Courier,* the most popular black community paper in the country.

"Yes, a sentimental one," Smith answered. "I'm from Detroit. He was the Tigers' shortstop when I was a boy. How about you? Who's your best?"

"Pop Lloyd." John Henry "Pop" Lloyd had played for over ten different teams in the Negro Leagues before moving over to managing in 1926.

Smith smiled. "Not Honus Wagner?" The Pittsburgh

Pirates player had been one of the first to be inducted into the Baseball Hall of Fame, back in 1936.

"Wagner is number two," Rickey told him. "And Rabbit Tavener would not break my top twenty-five. Where do you suppose Jackie Robinson will end up on that list?"

Smith shook his head. "He won't break it. He doesn't have a shortstop's arm. Robinson belongs on second base."

Rickey didn't seem bothered by that assessment. "All right, then, where would he rate at second?"

Smith considered. "If he was playing now, he'd be the best second baseman in the majors."

That won a smile from the Dodgers manager. "High praise. He'll have to be the best in the minor leagues first, though."

"What are you saying, Mr. Rickey?" Smith still wasn't entirely sure why Rickey had asked him to stop by.

Rickey's smile broadened. "I'm saying it's going to be a very interesting spring training. A lot of players are coming back from the war, and with gas rationing over, we can train down in Florida again."

"Daytona Beach?" Smith asked. "You're aware in the past six months a black boy was lynched in Madison and a black man down in Live Oak?"

Rickey waved that off. "Those towns may as well be a million miles from Daytona."

"Live Oak is one hundred and fifty, actually," Smith informed him.

"I spoke to the Daytona mayor," Rickey said. "He assures me there'll be no trouble." But he didn't sound entirely convinced himself. "Mr. Smith, are you a Communist?"

Smith laughed. "I'm a Democrat. Why do you ask?"

"I have a business proposition. What's your salary at the *Courier*?"

"Fifty dollars a week." It wasn't a lot, but it was enough for him. And it let him write about baseball.

Rickey nodded. "I will pay you an additional fifty dollars a week plus expenses if you will attend spring training with Jackie Robinson," he offered. "You will watch over him, help him to avoid the harm that could come if he were to do or say anything out of turn. You will act as his chauffeur, you will secure accommodations for him wherever the team may be, help him find restaurants, and so on."

"What's in it for me?" Smith asked. "Besides the fifty dollars and a whole lot of aggravation?"

Rickey's smile returned. "Unprecedented access to my team for any reporting you feel is appropriate. What do you say, Mr. Smith?"

Smith smiled back. "I say yes, sir. If a Negro is good enough

to stop a Nazi bullet in France, he's good enough to stop a line drive at Yankee Stadium."

"Ebbets Field actually," Rickey corrected. "But I believe you're right. The world is ready."

They shook hands, and Smith couldn't shake the feeling that he'd just agreed to participate in something wonderful.

CHAPTER 3

On February 28, 1946, Jackie's and Rachel's family and friends were on hand to see them off as they walked through the Burbank airport.

"You knock the cover off that ball," Jackie's mother, Mallie, urged him, blinking back proud tears.

"I will, Mama." He gave her a big hug, teary-eyed himself.

She hugged him back, then kissed Rachel. "Look after each other."

"We will," Rachel promised.

Mallie nodded, reached into her bag, and drew out a cardboard shoe box that was slightly greasy at the bottom. "Take this. It's chicken."

Jackie laughed. "They have food on the plane, Mama."

"You never know what might happen," Mallie insisted. "I don't want you getting there starving and too weak to hit."

Rachel caught Jackie's eye and shook her head ever so slightly. A few minutes later, he was escorting her onto the plane, the shoe box in hand.

"I couldn't tell her no," he protested weakly.

Rachel sighed. "I know she means well. I just don't want to be seen eating chicken out of a box like some country bumpkin."

Jackie smiled and ran a hand over her fancy new coat. "No one's going to mistake you for a bumpkin in this."

Rachel nodded proudly. "Well, they'll know I belong on that plane or wherever I happen to be."

Their argument forgotten, they stepped onto the gleaming plane.

When they landed for their first stopover, in New Orleans, Rachel headed straight for the nearest ladies' room, then stopped short. The sign on the door read "White Only."

Jackie was still carrying the box of chicken when he caught up to her. "The flight to Pensacola leaves in an hour," he started, then trailed off when he caught her expression. "You okay?"

She nodded. "I've just never seen one before."

Glancing over, Jackie saw the sign. "We're not in Pasadena

anymore." But Rachel didn't seem to hear him as she suddenly lurched into motion again—heading straight for the door. "Honey," he called after her. "Rae—" But she had already disappeared inside. Jackie glanced around, not sure what to do. Before, he would have done the same as her. But things were different now.

"I promised Mr. Rickey we'd stay out of trouble," he explained to her a few minutes later as they stepped into the airport's coffee shop.

"Did you promise him we wouldn't go to the bathroom?" she shot back. "You've snuck into segregated toilets before."

"*Before* I promised."

"It was just a toilet." She sniffed. "You'd think the commodes were made of gold."

They slid into the nearest empty booth, but just as they were reaching for the menu, the cook came bustling out of the kitchen. "You folks can't sit here," he told them.

Jackie glanced up. "Excuse me?"

"It's white only. I'll sell you some sandwiches," the cook continued, "but you gotta take 'em to go." He sounded like he felt bad about that.

Jackie started to say something, but stopped himself. Then he tried again. At least he wasn't picking a fight, as he would have done not long ago. "No," he answered instead. "You hang on to those." He stood up, glared at the cook, and offered Rachel his hand. She didn't say anything, but she was the very picture of outraged elegance as she accepted it and let him lead her away.

A few hours later, the plane landed in Pensacola, Florida, for refueling. There were only ten seats on the small plane, and when the door opened, four passengers departed. Four new people quickly took their places.

"Just a hop to Daytona now," Jackie assured Rachel. They were both exhausted from the long day of air travel. Their reception in New Orleans hadn't helped any

Rachel nodded, but motion by the plane door caught her eye as a woman entered. She was wearing an airline uniform. Her name tag read "Bishop."

The woman scanned the passengers, then made a beeline for them. "Jack Robinson?" she asked. "Come with me." She'd turned away before she'd even finished speaking, and glanced back impatiently when they didn't move immediately. "Come on now. Both of you."

Rachel looked at her husband. He shrugged and rose to his feet. "Guess we'd better do what she says," he commented. Rachel followed him out, but she had a bad feeling about this.

Once they were at the ticket counter, Miss Bishop explained.

"We have to lighten the plane. There's some bad weather east of here. A heavy plane's dangerous." They realized at once what she meant. They had been removed from their flight.

"Tell her you're with the Dodgers," Rachel urged quietly. But Jackie shrugged off the suggestion.

"When's the next flight?" he asked instead.

Miss Bishop smiled, but it was a phony one. "Tomorrow morning," she replied, "but it's booked. So someone'll have to cancel."

Jackie sighed. "Look, I'm with the Brooklyn Dodger organization. I've got to get down to Daytona. I'm supposed to report to spring training in the morning."

"We'll do our best to get you down there by tomorrow afternoon," Miss Bishop assured him stiffly, "but it might be the day after." Clearly the fact that he was with the Dodgers hadn't impressed her any.

Just then, Rachel noticed a couple being led out to their plane. A white couple. But there hadn't been any empty seats when they'd gotten up! Suddenly, she understood. "Jack—"

He followed her gaze, stared for a second, then wheeled on Miss Bishop, furious. "You gave away our seats! Get us back on that plane!" he demanded.

Instead she lifted the phone and held it between them. "Do you want to call the sheriff?" she asked nastily. "Or should I?"

That night, Rachel and Jackie sat in the deserted Pensacola train station. The bus right across from their bench read "Daytona Beach," but if wouldn't be leaving until the morning. Even though they were in Florida, it was chilly, and Rachel tugged her coat around her more tightly. She still couldn't believe what had happened to them. But there had been no fighting it, and after calming down she'd realized that. All arguing would have done was land them in jail, and wouldn't that be a lovely way for Jackie to start his new career?

Sitting next to her on the bench, Jackie stared off into the night. He'd known it would be tough, but he hadn't expected these difficulties to start so early. Nor had he realized that Rachel would get dragged into it with him. Leaning back, his hand brushed something at his side, and he glanced down. It was the shoe box. Reaching in, Jackie pulled out a drumstick, studied it for a second, then took a bite.

"Mama knew," he whispered.

He turned and offered the piece to his wife. She slid over, closing the gap between them, and took a bite. Then she smiled at him.

"It's good," she admitted. That was his Rachel, always looking for the bright side.

Jackie smiled back and wrapped his arm around her. As long as she was with him, he knew he'd be all right.

The next day, Rickey drove along a dirt road in Daytona Beach. He sang along with the radio as he passed Brooklyn Dodgers, Montreal Royals, and Saint Paul Saints, all warming up or already trading pitches, hits, and throws.

"How're they looking, Leo?" he asked as he stopped the car, got out, and walked over to where Dodgers coach Leo Durocher was hitting balls. Three of the Dodgers players, Pee Wee Reese, Eddie Stanky, and Dixie Walker were chasing the balls down.

"Rusty, Mr. Rickey," Durocher admitted. "But we'll get 'em oiled up and ready in no time. You find your lost sheep yet?"

Troubled, Rickey shook his head. Jackie and Rachel should have arrived the night before, but there'd been no sign of them on the plane. Just then, Parrott hurried over.

"Jackie Robinson's on a bus leaving Pensacola," he reported.

"A bus?" Rickey stared at him. "Harold, how in blazes did he end up on a bus?" Parrott shrugged. "Well, let Wendell know." Rickey saw a few of the other Dodgers—Bob Bragan, Ralph Branca, and Kirby Higbe—muttering to one another. He wondered if it was about Robinson, but shook off the thought.

Their first priority was getting him here. Then they'd figure out the rest.

"Jackie Robinson?" Jackie and Rachel glanced up. They'd been the last to stumble off the bus, even after the other black passengers, and they were surprised to see a round-faced, bespectacled black man waiting for them. "Mr. Rickey sent me to meet you." He offered his hand. "Wendell Smith, *Pittsburgh Courier*. I'm going to be your Boswell."

Jackie just stared. "My who?"

"Your chronicler, your advance man. Even your chauffeur." Smith tipped his hat. "Mrs. Robinson."

Rachel offered him a tired smile. "It's Rachel."

Smith regarded them both. "Man, you two look wiped out."

"You got a car?" Jackie asked, fatigue and frustration making the words come out sharper than he'd intended. "Get us out of here."

They carried the bags out to Smith's Buick. Along the way, Rachel couldn't help noticing that even the water fountains were segregated.

Smith caught her stare. "You ever been down South before, Rachel?"

She shook her head. “First time. We have our problems in Pasadena, but not like this.”

“Mr. Rickey says we follow the law,” Smith half-explained, half-warned. “If Jim Crow and the state of Florida say Negroes do this and that, then we do this and that.”

“My life’s changing right in front of me,” Rachel said softly, more to herself than to him. “Who I am, who I think I am.” She shook her head and climbed into the car.

“Joe and Duff Harris live here,” Smith explained when they finally pulled up in front of a handsome little house in Daytona Beach’s black neighborhood. “He gets out the black vote, does a lot of good for colored folks. Mr. Rickey set it up himself.” He deepened his voice in a fair imitation of Rickey: “‘If we can’t put the Robinsons in the hotels, they should stay someplace that represents something.’”

Jackie and Rachel exchanged a look, unsure whether to laugh or not. At least the place seemed nice.

“Brooklyn plays downtown,” Smith continued. “Montreal a few blocks from here. You’ll stay with the Harrises except for a few days at the end of the week. The whole Dodger organization is going to Sanford, about forty-five minutes away. Rachel, you’ll remain here.”

"Where are the other wives staying?" she asked.

Smith laughed. "There are no other wives. You're the only one Mr. Rickey allowed to spring training."

A friendly looking couple stepped out onto the porch and waved hello, and Rachel automatically waved back.

"I hope you like it," Mrs. Harris told them as she led them up the stairs to a door at the very top.

"I'm sure we will," Rachel promised her. "Thank you." They'd only been there a few minutes, but she already liked the Harrises.

"Dinner's at five," Mrs. Harris told them as she headed back down. Jackie had already stepped into the room, and Rachel followed him, closing the door behind her—then accidentally knocked Jackie onto the bed. The room was so small that, between the bed and their luggage, there wasn't even any room to move!

"It's a joke, right?" Jackie asked. He gazed about them in disbelief.

But Rachel smiled. "I like it." She'd fallen on top of him, and now she kissed him soundly. He smiled and wrapped his arms around her. "Remind me dinner's at five," she warned.

He laughed. "I'll try to remember." Then he hugged her close. They'd unpack later. Once they'd had a chance to forget all about planes and trains, and even baseball.

CHAPTER 4

he next morning, Smith pulled up at the training field alongside the team buses. He glanced over at Jackie. This was the first time he'd seen the young ballplayer nervous.

"The first day of spring training," he said gently. "My *Pittsburgh Courier* readers need to know how it feels."

Jackie shrugged. "It's okay."

"That's not exactly a headline," Smith pointed out.

"That's all I got." Jackie didn't look at him. He stared down at his hands instead. They were clenched together tightly.

Smith shook his head. "Look, Jack, right now it's just me asking you. But you get on that field and it's going to be the *New York Times* and the *Sporting News*. You should think about it."

"If they ask something, I'll answer," Jackie told him pointedly. He didn't mean to snap at Smith, but this day was so important, he let his nerves get the better of him.

"All right," Smith tried again, "but you know when you're at the plate, you want to feel like you see the pitch come in slow? Well, you want to see the questions come in slow, too."

Jackie didn't say anything. He just glared at him for a second, then climbed out of the car. Smith watched him walk away, and sighed.

Out by the field, Rickey was sitting on one of the benches, fuming. When Parrott hurried over, Rickey shook a newspaper at him.

"Listen to this, Harold," he declared. He pulled the paper open and began to read from it: "'Whenever I hear a white man'—yours truly—'broadcasting what a Moses he is to the Negro race, then I know the latter needs a bodyguard. It is those of the carpetbagger stripe of the white race'—me again—'who, under the guise of helping, in truth are using the Negro for their own selfish interest, thereby retarding the race!'" He growled and crumpled the paper in his hands. "The minor league commissioner of baseball said that! I pay part of his salary! *You* wouldn't stab me in the back like this, would you?"

Parrott shook his head, then finally managed to get a word in. "He's here, Mr. Rickey."

"He is?" Rickey rose to his feet at once. "Why didn't you say so?"

Out on the field, two hundred white players stopped what they were doing as Jackie crossed the field, wearing his brand-new Montreal Royals uniform and carrying a glove and a bat. Reporters and photographers surrounded him immediately, and the burst of flashbulbs going off left Jackie reeling and partially blinded. Everyone was shouting questions at once, and Jackie had to concentrate to break them apart into coherent sentences.

"Jackie," one reporter called, "do you think you can make it with these white boys?"

Jackie looked around, seeking help—and spotted Smith standing behind the others, just watching. He remembered what the other man had said. *See the questions slow.* So he took a deep breath, let it out, and used that second to think so he could answer clearly: "Sure, I had no problem with white men in the service or at UCLA."

"What'll you do if one of these pitchers throws at your head?" someone else asked.

Jackie gave himself a second before replying, "I'll duck."

That got some laughs.

"Jack, what's your natural position?" a third reporter called.

At least that one was easy. "I've been playing shortstop."

But then the same man followed up with "Are you after Pee Wee Reese's job?"

Jackie looked over and spotted Reese watching with another Dodger he recognized, Ed Stanky. "Reese plays for Brooklyn," he answered. "I'm worried about making Montreal."

The first reporter hurled another question. "Is this about politics?"

Jackie shook his head and smiled. "It's about getting paid." He saw Smith smile and nod, and relaxed a little. He could do this.

Rickey had held back—this was Jackie's moment, not his. But now, as the first barrage of questions died down a bit, he cut in, smiling and nodding as he drew Jackie away and led him across the field to where a middle-aged man in a Royals uniform waited. "Clay," he said as they reached the man, "I'd like you to meet Jackie Robinson. Jackie, Clay Hopper, manager of the Montreal Royals."

Hopper held out his hand. "We ain't doing much today," he told Jackie, and though there was a clear Southern drawl to his words, his voice and manner sounded neutral, maybe even a little bit friendly. "Just throwing the ball around and hitting

a few. Why don't you toss a few with those fellas over there?" He turned toward a kid in a Royals uniform. "Hey, Jorgensen!" The kid looked up. "Meet Jackie Robinson."

By the end of the day, Jackie was tired, but feeling pretty good. He'd held his own with the Montreal players, and if some of them hadn't warmed much to him, others had accepted him as just another guy on the team. And that was all he wanted.

Two of the Dodgers called out to him, however, as he walked past the buses to where Smith and his Buick waited.

"Hey, rook!" one of them, Higbe, shouted. "Did you hear about the redneck shortstop?"

The other, Bragan, followed up: "He thought the last two words of the national anthem were 'play ball'!"

Jackie managed a smile, but he couldn't help wondering if they were heckling because he was the new guy or because he was black.

Higbe tried again: "How about the shortstop making all the errors who tried to kill himself by jumping out on the highway?"

And Bragan finished the joke, "A bus just missed him. Drove right between his legs!"

A few of the other players laughed as the pair climbed onto the Dodgers bus and it pulled away. Most of the faces staring down at him glared or looked at him blankly. Only one, the young pitcher Ralph Branca, smiled and waved.

"'Between his legs,' good one," Smith muttered as Jackie reached him. "He must've read a joke book. If he can read." Jackie just climbed in the car without a word. Smith sighed, then beat a quick drumroll on the hood of the Buick. "Hi, Wendell, how are you?" he asked, then glanced over at his silent passenger and sighed again. "Well, looks like I got a long drive to Sanford."

XXX

It was almost evening when they pulled up in front of the Brock house in Sanford. Mr. Brock stepped out onto the front porch to meet them. He was carrying a tray of tall drinks, the glasses glistening with condensation.

"Jackie," he said as they reached him, setting the tray on a table so he could offer his hand, "I'm Ray Brock. Welcome to Sanford, Florida! The day belongs to decent-minded people." He turned to Smith next. "Wendell, good to see you.

"My wife's inside, cooking," Brock added after the greetings were over. "You know what she asked me this morning? She asked me, 'What do you serve when a hero's coming for dinner?'"

Jackie scuffed his feet, not used to such attention. "I'm just a ballplayer, Mr. Brock."

But Brock laughed good-naturedly. "Tell that to all the little colored boys playing baseball in Florida today. You're a hero to them." He gestured toward the tray, the table, and the rocking chairs beside them. "Sit down, have something to drink. My special rum and Coke."

But Jackie shook his head. "No thank you, sir. I don't drink." Even if he had before, he wouldn't now—there was no way he was going to let anyone paint a picture of him as a lush!

"A ballplayer who doesn't drink?" Brock let out a low whistle, then shook his head. "That's a new one on me."

"I'll have one," Smith was quick to offer. "I'm a stereotypical reporter through and through."

All three of them laughed.

"Mr. Brock," Jackie asked, "do you have a desk? I'd like to get a letter to my wife."

Brock clapped him on the shoulder. "Of course, this way." He led Jackie inside, while Smith settled into one of the chairs and claimed one of the drinks. Jackie could tell already that, except for Rachel being back in Daytona Beach, he was going to like it here.

The next day, Rickey and Hopper watched the training game between Montreal and Saint Paul. Jackie was playing second.

"He's getting by on a quick release," Hopper commented, "but his arm's too weak for short. Second base is his spot."

"I agree." Rickey frowned. "And I'll state another obvious, Clay—I need the players to act like gentlemen around him." Hopper just nodded, not taking his eyes off the field. "To treat him as they would any other teammate. To be natural, to impose no restrictions on themselves. To all work together in harmony."

The whack of a bat solidly connecting made him look up, as a low line drive shot for the gap between first and second. Jackie lunged forward, glove outstretched, and snagged the ball before it could hit the ground. Then he spun around and dropped to one knee, firing the ball back to first before the runner who'd just left there could make it back safely. It was a beautiful play.

"That was superhuman," Rickey whispered, awed.

Next to him, Hopper chuckled. "Superhuman? Don't get carried away, Mr. Rickey. That's still a nigger out there."

The offhanded comment, and the casual, everyday tone of it, stunned Rickey more than the play had, and it took him a second to process it. He'd known that Hopper was originally from Mississippi, but had just assumed his time in Montreal had worn away any rough edges from his childhood. Finally, however, Rickey found his voice again and said, "Clay, I realize that attitude is part of your heritage, that you practically nursed race prejudice at your mother's breast, so I will let it pass. But I will add this: You can manage Robinson fairly and correctly, or you can be unemployed."

Hopper didn't reply directly. He didn't even give any sign he'd heard his boss's reprimand. But as Jackie headed off the field toward them, he called out, "Attaboy, Jackie! Way to turn two!"

Rickey nodded. That would do.

Late that night, the phone rang in Rickey's hotel room. He sat up and answered, listening for a second as the caller identified himself. "Yes, Wendell, what is it?"

"A guy just stopped by the Brocks' house," Smith explained hurriedly. "Said there were fellas coming who weren't too happy about Jackie's being here. About him playing with white boys. And that it'd be best if we weren't here when they arrived."

Rickey frowned, though there was no one there to notice it. "I see. Yes, I understand. Wake him up and get him out of there. Put him in the car and start driving for Daytona Beach. Now. And, Wendell, under no circumstance tell him what this is about. I do not want him to get it in his head to stay there and fight."

After they hung up, Rickey shook his head, then sighed and

rose to his feet. He knew he wasn't likely to get any more sleep that night.

Back at the Brocks', Jackie sat on the edge of his bed, half-dressed and only half-awake. Through his door he could see Smith in his own room across the hall, quickly packing his things.

"I was just getting loose," Jackie muttered to himself, shaking his head. He couldn't believe the dream was over that quickly.

Smith stuck his head in the doorway. "Don't just sit there; pack your duds. We're blowin'."

A phone rang somewhere downstairs. They heard Brock answer, then call up, "Wendell?"

Smith headed down, and Jackie listened as the sportswriter took the phone.

"Yes, Mr. Rickey," he heard Smith say, "I'm with him now. We're pulling out for Daytona in five minutes, soon as he gets his bag packed. Yes, yes, it's just one of those things."

Jackie hung his head. "One of those things." Not to him, it wasn't.

They left quickly, barely pausing to thank the Brocks for their hospitality. The road was quiet at this time of night, with

only a few bars still open. One of those stood at a street corner, and as they braked to a stop, Jackie saw a pickup idling there in its parking lot. A dozen men in shirtsleeves emerged from the bar to speak with the men in the truck. Then one of them glanced up and spotted the Buick and its passengers. He marched over, gesturing for Jackie to roll down the window.

"I wonder what he wants?" Jackie said aloud, already reaching for the window crank.

"To run us out of town," Smith answered.

Jackie turned to look at him. "What are you talking about?"

The man was close now, and Jackie had the window open a crack when Smith suddenly floored it, sending the Buick shooting away with a loud screech. Another car was coming from the other direction, and Smith had to swerve to keep from hitting it.

"Seriously, Wendell?" Jackie found he was shaking a little.

Smith let out a breath, checked the mirror, and slowed down. "Man came by while you were asleep," he explained. "Told us more men were coming. Maybe those boys. Mr. Rickey said to get you to Daytona Beach ASAP."

Jackie stared at him. "Why didn't you say so?"

Smith shrugged. "Mr. Rickey was afraid you wouldn't leave, that you'd want to fight."

Instead of getting angry, Jackie started to laugh.

"What are you laughing at?" Smith demanded, his own fear making him snappish.

It took a second for Jackie to control himself enough to answer. "I thought you woke me because I was cut from the team."

After a second, Smith started laughing with him. But as they drove on and the irony faded, Jackie found himself glancing back over his shoulder. *How much worse can it get?* he wondered.

CHAPTER 5

few days later, the City Island Ball Park hosted a game between the Dodgers and the Royals. Hundreds of people, a large portion of Daytona Beach's black community, turned out to see Jackie play.

In the Dodgers dugout, Rickey munched on a bag of peanuts and gave voice to his thoughts, with only the team's batboy to hear them.

"I've spoken to the mayor," he told the boy. "I've explained how much money we'll spend in Daytona. But still, when this fine young Negro man steps on that field today, he and the Dodgers will technically be breaking the law. A law which says white and black players cannot enjoy the same field at the

same time. Does that make sense to you? Does Jim Crow make any sense when placed against the words of the United States Constitution? When placed against the word of God?" He shook his head. "I'll tell you, it does not make sense to me."

The young batboy wisely didn't say anything at all.

Jackie stood in the on-deck circle, swinging two bats to loosen up. He watched as the Montreal batter ahead of him hit a line drive, and Pee Wee Reese sprang into the air like a bullet to take it down. No question about it, he was playing in the big leagues now.

As he stepped up to the plate, the announcer called out the words he'd been waiting to hear, "Now batting, the second baseman—Jackie Robinson!"

There was a mix of cheers and boos from the white sections, but the packed black section offered him a standing ovation, and Jackie couldn't help but smile as he took his place and raised his bat.

"Come on, black boy," someone called from the white sections, "you can make the grade!"

Another added, "They're giving you a chance! Do something about it!"

Jackie nodded. He could do this. He concentrated on

Higbe's first pitch—then had to jerk out of the way to avoid getting hit by it.

Bragan, the catcher, chucked the ball back. Jackie could feel the man looking up at him, but refused to take his eyes off the mound. He remembered Bragan's and Higbe's jokes that first day, but he wasn't going to think about that now. He was here to play.

Higbe fired again, even tighter than before, missing Jackie by an inch.

"Ball two!" the umpire called.

The third pitch was way outside, and Jackie didn't move a muscle as it sailed by. Ball three.

"Come on, rook!" Higbe taunted. "Ain't you gonna swing at something?"

Sure, Jackie thought to himself. *Just give me something worth swinging at.* He took a practice swing to show Higbe he could, then got back into position and waited. This time, the pitch was too low. Ball four.

A cheer from the colored section followed him all the way to first—and then turned to stunned silence as Jackie took a deliberately large lead off the bag. Higbe stared at him for a second.

"Well, throw over there, for crying out loud!" the Dodgers coach, Leo Durocher, commanded from the dugout.

Higbe obeyed, firing a fastball to Lavagetto. Jackie dove back just in time.

When the pitcher turned away, Jackie took a lead off the bag again, though he settled for a more modest one this time. As soon as Higbe loosed the ball toward home, however, Jackie was off and running. Bragan saw him, of course, and hurled the ball to Pee Wee, but it was late and high and Jackie made it to the bag safely. He didn't even have to slide.

He could see that Higbe was upset as Pee Wee tossed the ball back to him. Well, too bad. And as soon as Higbe threw his next pitch, Jackie took off again, this time gunning for third. But Bragan's toss beat him there, and now Jackie was caught between players as the Dodgers tried to run him down. Good thing none of them had his speed! It was Higbe who finally came after him near the bag—and Jackie ducked under the attempted tag and managed to get a hand on third. Safe!

The entire stadium was buzzing now, and as he dusted himself off, Jackie could see Rickey pounding one fist into the other with excitement. He hoped the general manager felt he was getting his money's worth.

Jackie stepped off third as Higbe returned to the mound. How closely was the Dodgers pitcher watching him? He feinted toward home, and Higbe took a step toward him. Normally, a

player who was on base would head back at that, but Jackie held his ground.

"You're supposed to go back to third when I step off!" Higbe shouted at him. "Don't you know nothing?" He threw the ball, but Jackie beat it back easily. Then, as soon as Higbe turned away, he stepped off again. He rocked back and forth, getting ready.

Apparently, his restlessness unsettled Higbe. The pitcher started his delivery, glanced around, caught a glimpse of Jackie bouncing on his feet—and dropped the ball. The umpire spotted it and signaled a balk. Then he pointed Jackie home. *Yes!*

It wasn't the way Jackie had wanted to score, but he'd settle for throwing Higbe off his game. This time. The colored section went wild with cheering as he sauntered across home plate. "Look at me, Ma," he whispered as he reached the dugout. "Playing baseball with the white boys. And scoring offa 'em, too! Not too shabby!"

A week later, though, Jackie wasn't having quite as good a time. The team was in DeLand, Florida, playing Indianapolis. It was the top of the first, no score, and Jackie had just dropped a bunt straight down the first base line. The first baseman fielded the ball too late to tag Jackie, so he tossed it to the second

baseman—who was too far out to cover his own base. The ball sailed by him, so Jackie put his head down and made it to second base safely. It was a bunt double, and the packed colored section went wild.

Spider Jorgensen was up to bat next and cracked a single out to left field. Jackie took the opportunity to race to third—and there was Sukeforth, waving him home. Jackie wasn't about to argue.

He raced toward home plate, the catcher already bracing himself for the throw, but the ball wasn't in his glove yet when Jackie barreled into him and landed on the base. Safe!

But as he clambered back to his feet, Jackie found himself facing not an umpire but a cop. A big, angry cop who grabbed him by the shoulder.

"Git offa this field now!" the cop bellowed at him.

Jackie stared at him. "What? Why?"

"It's against the law is why," the cop snarled back. "Niggers don't play with no white boys. Git off or go to jail."

Jackie shrugged the policeman's hand off his shoulder, and the cop reached for his nightstick just as Sukeforth joined them.

"You swing that thing, you better hit me between the eyes with it," Jackie warned, balling his fists. Promise or no promise, he wasn't about to stand meekly while somebody tried to beat him down.

The cop narrowed his eyes. "Is that so?" The booing from the stands—most, but not all of it from the black section—almost drowned him out.

Just then, Hopper burst from the dugout. "Hey, hold on," he demanded, "what'd he do wrong?"

"We ain't havin' Nigras mix with white boys in this town," the cop informed him coldly. "Ya'll ain't up-states now; they gotta stay separate. Brooklyn Dodgers ain't changin' our way of living. Where are y'all from, anyhow?"

"Greenwood, Mississippi," Hopper answered.

The cop sneered down at him. "You oughta know better. Now tell your Nigra I said to git. You think I'm foolin'?"

Hopper looked over at Jackie, who hadn't budged. Now what?

"What did you do?" Rachel asked breathlessly. It was evening now, and the Robinsons were taking a walk before dinner. Jackie had been telling her the story, since she hadn't made it to the game that day.

He shook his head—and then he grinned. "I said, 'Okay, Skipper, tell him Ah'm a-gittin'. Sho'nuff, Ah is.'"

Rachel laughed delightedly, one hand going to her mouth. "You didn't?"

"I did. Then I took a long shower." His grin faded. "We lost two to one."

Seeing his mood darken, Rachel took several exaggeratedly slow steps. "Ah'm a-gittin'," she drawled, "Ah'm a-gittin'."

That did it, and he laughed, taking her hand again and pulling her close. "You're not getting away from me," he warned playfully.

Rachel smiled, but then she happened to glance over his shoulder. A white man had appeared on the far side of the street, and he was making a beeline for them. "Jack . . ."

Jackie turned, spotted the man, and quickly shifted around, putting Rachel behind him. "Get back, Rae. Go back." His whole body was tense, coiled and ready for action.

The man, clearly a local, stopped right in front of Jackie and stared at him. "I want you to know something," he announced in a thick Florida drawl.

"Yeah?" Jackie asked. "What's that?"

The man smiled. "I want you to know I'm pulling for you to make good. And a lot of folks here feel the same way. If a man's got the goods, he deserves a fair chance. That's all." Then he tipped his hat to Rachel. "Ma'am."

"Well, how about that?" Jackie said softly as they watched the man leave. "How do you like that?"

Rachel smiled. "I like it just fine."

The training season sped past, and soon enough Rickey found himself leaning against his car on the last day, watching a groundskeeper mow the infield grass. He looked up as Jackie joined him. It felt strange to see the young ballplayer in street clothes after so many weeks in uniform.

"You wanted to see me, Mr. Rickey?" Jackie asked.

Rickey nodded. He glanced back out over the training field. "Bermuda grass grows so well here," he remarked. "I wish we could get it to grow like this in Brooklyn."

Beside him, Jackie nodded. "I like the way it smells when they mow it."

"Me, too." Rickey considered the field a moment, then turned back to Jackie. "Jackie, it's my pleasure to tell you that you've earned a spot on the Montreal Royals. When they head north Tuesday for opening day against Jersey City, you'll be on the train."

Jackie nodded, but Rickey could tell he was trying to contain his excitement. He was still so young!

"I won't let you down," Jackie promised after a minute.

Rickey smiled and offered his hand. "I know that."

They shook, and then Jackie stepped away. "If you don't mind, I've got to go tell my wife."

Rickey nodded. "Give her my regards." He hadn't spent much time with Rachel Robinson, but what he had seen of her he admired. She was poised, graceful, smart, and supportive—exactly what Jackie needed. And it was obvious the young couple doted on each other.

Jackie had only gone a few paces before he glanced back. "Why are you doing this, Mr. Rickey?" he asked.

"I'm an opportunist," Rickey replied easily. "With you and the Negro players I hope to bring up next year, I'll put together a team that can win the World Series. And the World Series means money." As he paused, he caught the frown that flashed across Jackie's face. "Don't you believe that?"

"I don't think what I believe is important," Jackie answered after a moment. "Only what I do."

Rickey nodded. "Agreed. Now worry those pitchers until they come apart. Sometimes they'll catch you, but don't worry about that. Ty Cobb got caught plenty. Just run as you see fit. Put the natural fear of God into them."

Jackie smiled. "I can do that."

As Jackie walked away, Rickey smiled as well. "Yes, you can," he agreed.

CHAPTER 6

April 18, 1946. A clear, beautiful day in Jersey City. Perfect for opening day of the International League season. Thirty thousand fans had packed into Roosevelt Stadium, filling it to capacity and beyond. Several thousand of those were black, and up here in the North they sat anywhere they could afford, not segregated into Colored and White sections. Flags and banners decorated the stadium, and everyone was in a festive mood. Except, perhaps, for the nervous young man stepping up to the plate.

Jackie was still unable to believe he was really here. Playing baseball in the minor leagues! The *white* minor leagues! He heard a few boos as he raised his bat, but there were a lot more cheers, and a lot more shouts of encouragement than catcalls.

"Come on, Jackie!" one fan yelled from the stands. "This fella can't pitch!"

Jackie smiled and raised his bat, but he was still unable to focus. He connected on the first pitch, but not well, knocking a weak grounder almost right into the shortstop's glove. He ran for first anyway, but the toss beat him there by a mile. *Not the best start,* he thought as he turned and jogged back toward the dugout. Still, it was only the first inning.

Up in the stands, over by third, Rachel sat next to Smith, who held his typewriter balanced on his lap, ready and waiting. But Jackie's first at bat was hardly something worth writing about. Smith gathered that Rachel felt the same way—she looked ill, and held a hand up to her mouth.

"You okay?" he asked her. He'd come to like Rachel Robinson. He liked her husband, too, even if he was prickly most of the time.

Normally, Rachel would have waved off his concern, but not this time. "I think I might be sick," she admitted, rising to her feet. "Excuse me, Wendell." She carefully made her way along the row, toward the nearest exit.

Smith watched her go. "I'd be sick at a swing like that, too," he muttered, looking to where Jackie had just slumped

onto the bench. Smith knew the newest Montreal player had to be anxious, which explained his poor showing just now. It wasn't a surprise that his pretty, young wife had a case of the nerves to match.

Rachel knew it was more than nerves, and made it to the ladies' room just in time. After emptying her stomach, she stepped to the sink and splashed some water on her face. An older black woman at the next sink watched her, sympathy written in every line of her face.

"Are you all right, honey?" she asked.

Rachel shook her head. "I'm sick. I don't know why." She'd actually been feeling nauseous and light-headed for several days now, but she hadn't wanted to say anything. Jackie was under enough pressure as it was.

The woman handed her a paper towel, and Rachel thanked her. "It may be that you're pregnant," the older lady suggested. She smiled, patted Rachel on the arm, and then left her alone with her thoughts.

Rachel stared at herself in the mirror. Pregnant? Now? When Jackie was just starting out here? What would he say? What would they do?

But she felt a flutter of excitement, too. She was pregnant!

Rachel stepped out onto the runway leading back to the seats just as the announcer called, "Now batting—Jackie Robinson!" Hurrying her steps, Rachel reached the end of the tunnel and stopped, looking out over the railing across the field. There he was, standing tall at home plate, bat in hand. He looked confident and in control, and she could tell from here that he'd fought off his first-day jitters—his gaze was clear and sharp. Just seeing him there made her feel better. She stood and watched, one hand unconsciously grazing her belly, as he settled down and lifted the bat to his shoulder.

The pitcher peered over one shoulder at the Montreal runner on first, then over the other at the one on second. Then he turned his eyes back toward home plate. He tensed, his whole body coiled like a spring. And just as quickly, he unleashed all his energy, hurling the ball forward like a shot from a cannon. It was a high fastball—and Jackie caught it dead-on with a massive *CRACK!* The ball sailed across left field, out over the stands, before finally slamming into the scoreboard and bouncing away.

"Oh, Jack!" Rachel said softly, clapping her hands together. And she wasn't the only one. All around her, people were cheering and shouting and clapping as Jackie trotted around the bases. He wasn't in any hurry, especially with his two teammates making their way ahead of him. Both of them turned and waited for him once they'd crossed home plate, and shook his hand as he joined them. Rachel could see Jackie was beaming, and so was she. If ever there had been any doubts that this was the right place for him to be, they were gone now, erased like they had never existed. This was where he belonged, out on this field with these players—these white players, and maybe someday other black players, too.

"Oh, Jack!" Rachel said again as she turned back toward the tunnel. She started down it, trying to figure out how to best make her way down to her husband. He was going to be in a good mood—one she hoped would continue when he found out that a few months from now their lives might be changing again.

Rachel cried out from the delivery room of Huntington Memorial Hospital. It was November 18, and they had come back to Pasadena for their baby to be born—Jackie had declared that if California had been good enough for him and for her, it was good enough for their child. Labor pains stabbed through her abdomen, but soon enough they had passed, and she found the doctor offering her a wriggling little bundle, all scrunched-up face and wide, wailing mouth.

"Congratulations," he told her happily. "It's a boy!"

Rachel held out her arms for her son, exhausted and happy.

That night, Jackie stood outside the maternity ward,

looking in at his son. Jack Robinson Jr. lay nestled in his bassinet, swaddled carefully, his eyes closed in blissful, untroubled sleep. He was beautiful.

Jackie leaned against the glass and stared. He hadn't known many babies, but he couldn't imagine any of them being more perfect. He still remembered when Rachel had told him she was pregnant, right after that big hit in the game against Jersey City. He'd been on top of the world already, but finding out he was going to be a father? That had sent him truly soaring.

He was nervous, of course. It was a big responsibility. But Jackie knew one thing for certain: He was ready for it.

"My daddy left," he said softly, as if Jackie Junior could hear him. "He left us flat in Cairo, Georgia. I was only six months older than you are now. I don't remember him. Nothing good, nothing bad. Nothing." He spread his hand wide and pressed it against the glass. "But you're going to remember me," he promised his newborn son. "And I am going to be with you until the day I die."

Standing there, he remembered what Mr. Rickey had said to him, that first day in his office. "A man needs a family relying on him. It ensures he'll behave responsibly." Jackie finally understood that. Because from now on, he knew everything he did would be to make his little boy proud. He hoped he could live up to that. He was definitely going to give it his absolute best shot.

CHAPTER 7

wo months into the new year, on February 5, Rickey sat in the front row of a packed room at the Brooklyn YMCA, waiting for his turn to speak. Herbert Miller, a leading member of Brooklyn's black community and the executive secretary of the local YMCA, was introducing him, but Rickey was more interested in two deacons who sat nearby, whispering over the sports page.

"Look here what he did," one of them said. He read from the paper: "'Led the International League in batting: three forty-nine; in stolen bases: forty; runs scored: one hundred thirteen. Plus, batted four hundred in the Minor League World Series.'"

But the other deacon shook his head. "Last season doesn't matter. The International League, it doesn't matter. What matters is this year. What matters is Brooklyn." Rickey privately agreed.

Just then he heard Miller say, "I present the general manager of the Brooklyn Dodgers Baseball Club, Mr. Branch Rickey!"

Rickey smiled, stood, and stepped forward, accepting the podium from Miller. Looking out at the crowd, he saw thirty or so men gathered before him, all of them important figures in the local black community. These were the people he'd come here to see. These were the people he had to reach tonight.

"Good evening," he began. "I have something very important to talk with you about tonight. Something that will require courage from all of us." He paused for a second. "I have a ballplayer on my Montreal farm team named Jackie Robinson." That won him a burst of applause, but Rickey motioned them to silence. "He may stay there or he may be brought to Brooklyn. But if Jackie does come up to the Dodgers, the biggest threat to his success, the one enemy most likely to ruin that success, is the Negro people themselves!"

That caused a wave of stunned silence, followed by a few whispers—but not from the men in chairs. Glancing around, Rickey realized that there was a raised running track circling the room, and a group of boys were gathered there, eavesdropping. He bit back a smile. That was fine. The more people who heard him now, the better.

But he wasn't going to pull any punches, kids or no kids. "I say it as cruelly as I can," he stated loudly, "to make you all consider the weight of responsibility that is felt not only by me and the Dodgers, but by Negroes everywhere. Because on the day Jackie enters the National League, if he ever does, I have no doubt every one of you will throw parades and form welcoming committees. You'll strut. You'll wear badges. You'll hold Jackie Robinson days and Jackie Robinson nights. You'll get drunk, fight, and get arrested."

Now Rickey heard angry mutterings among the men as they registered those insults, but Rickey wasn't about to let that stop him. "You'll wine and dine him," he accused, "until he is fat and futile. You'll turn his importance into a national comedy and, yes, a tragedy! So let me tell you this!" He pounded his fist on the lectern, underscoring the intensity of his desire to make this group see how crucial it was to avoid distracting Jackie from the game. "If any group or segment of Negro society uses the advancement of Jackie Robinson in baseball as a triumph of race over race, I will regret the day I ever signed him to a contract, and I will personally see to it that baseball is never so abused and misrepresented again!"

Having finished what he came to say, Rickey turned and walked off the small stage. He kept going, through the door and out into the hallway, where he leaned against the wall and

let himself take several deep, gulping breaths. He had been harsh, yes, but had he gotten through to them? Did they understand? Could they see past their own hurt pride, past petty revenge, to what had to be done if Jackie Robinson was to have any career at all?

The sound of approaching footsteps made him straighten just as Miller stepped through the door and joined him. Miller didn't look pleased, exactly, but Rickey didn't think he looked furious, either.

They stood there in silence for a moment, and then Miller sighed and shook his head. "I question your bedside manner, Mr. Rickey," he commented, "but they've agreed to set up a committee of self-policing. We'll call it the 'Don't Spoil Jackie's Chances' campaign."

Rickey nodded and offered his hand. They had listened after all! "Thank you, Mr. Miller," he said. "I'm sorry; the spotlight will be on us."

As they shook hands, Rickey allowed himself to feel a tiny twinkling of hope. This just might work after all!

Jackie stood in front of the cozy house on Pepper Street, holding his little boy and kissing him good-bye. After a second, he handed the cooing baby off to his mother, who received a kiss from Jackie as well before she headed back inside. As the cabbie carried his bags out to his taxi, Jackie turned to Rachel, alone at last.

"Promise me you'll write," Rachel demanded. It killed her that she couldn't go to Florida with him this time, but Jackie Junior was still too young to travel that far safely. It would be better for him if they stayed here, with Jackie's mother. Better for him, but not for her.

Jackie gave her a smile. "When did I ever not write?" he asked gently.

But Rachel wasn't about to let him blow her off. "I want you to know I'm there for you," she explained. "Even if it's words on paper."

Jackie took her in his arms, holding her tight against his chest. "Rae, you're in my heart." She could hear it thudding, as if confirming that was true.

Even so, she sighed. "You're getting close now," she warned him. "The closer you get, the worse they'll be. Don't let them get to you."

"I will not," he promised. "God built me to last."

He pulled back just far enough to kiss her, and she returned the kiss fiercely.

"See you in Brooklyn in eight weeks," Rachel said when they finally broke for air.

Jackie frowned. "It might be Montreal."

But Rachel didn't believe that, not for a second. "It's going to be Brooklyn," she told him. "I know it is."

Jackie nodded, though he didn't seem convinced. The taxi honked, and he glanced toward it, then back at her. "I've got to go, Rae."

She nodded and hugged him one last time, then stood back and watched him head toward the waiting car. But she just couldn't let him go that easily. When after a second Jackie stopped and looked back at her, she flew toward him, and soon he was catching her in his arms, squeezing her tight. She didn't want to see him go, and she knew he didn't want to leave her. But he had to, at least for now.

"Go," she told him. "I'll be right here for you. Go, and hit one out of the park for me."

He smiled at her again, and it showered a warm glow of light upon her heart. "Rae, I'll hit every one out of the park for you."

CHAPTER 8

t's a pipe dream, Mr. Rickey." Durocher and his boss were eating at the Tivoli Hotel in Panama City. At least, Durocher was eating. Rickey had barely touched his food. It was March 18, 1947. Spring training was just about to start, and they were talking about the most distinctive and controversial player in their organization. Sometimes Rickey thought Jackie was all he ever talked about anymore.

Right now he was staring at his top coach. "Is that your attitude toward Jackie Robinson?"

Durocher groaned. "I don't got an attitude toward him. I'll play an elephant if he can help us win. To make room for him, I'll send my own brother home if he's not as good. We're

playing for money, Mr. Rickey," Durocher said. "Winning's the only thing that matters. Is he a nice guy?"

Rickey chuckled. "If by 'nice' you mean soft, no, not particularly."

Durocher nodded. "Good. He can't afford to be. Nice guys finish last."

"So, you have no objections to him?" Rickey asked.

"None whatsoever," Durocher managed to reply.

"So, why do you think this is a pipe dream?" Rickey liked Durocher, even if he had an eye for the ladies. He admired the man's willingness to stand up and speak his mind, but sometimes that forthrightness got on his nerves.

"I mean it ain't gonna happen," Durocher explained. "The Dodgers are never gonna demand Robinson be brought up from Montreal. Ballplayers are conservative."

Rickey shook his head. "A team full of tough war veterans? Immigrants' sons? Boys from impoverished corners of the country?" If any team was likely to accept a black player among them, it would be his Dodgers!

But Durocher just shrugged. "It. Ain't. Gonna. Happen."

"You really believe they won't accept him?" Rickey asked. "Once they see how he plays, how he can help them win?"

The coach laughed. "I'm not saying they won't accept him: I'm saying they won't ask for him. I'm saying Robinson's good

medicine, but they're not gonna like the taste." He shoved another forkful of food into his mouth. "Boy, this is good fish."

Rickey just sat and watched him eat. He had a sinking suspicion Durocher might be right.

In another room at the hotel, a few of Durocher's Dodgers were gathered around a small desk. One of them, Higbe, was writing something on a piece of hotel stationery while his teammates Bragan, Walker, and Hugh Casey looked on. All of them were veterans of the team, and what's more, all of them originally hailed from the South.

"Why do you think Rickey's got us playing spring games in Panama?" Alabama-born Bragan asked the others. "He wants to get us used to Negro crowds. He wants more of them than us. He's hoping it'll get us more comfortable being around Robinson."

Higbe, who was from South Carolina, cleared his throat. The others stopped their chatter, and then he read them what he'd written: "We, the undersigned Brooklyn Dodgers, will not play ball on the same field as Jackie Robinson."

He signed it and handed the pen to Bragan, who added his name. Georgia boy Casey signed it next, with a flourish. He

offered the pen to Walker, who, like Bragan, was from Alabama, but Walker didn't take it right away.

The others looked at one another. They knew the more names they had, the more power their petition would hold. And Walker was one of the mainstays of the team. His name carried weight.

Casey waved the pen. "If you wanna make your mark, Dixie," he joked, "we can witness it."

They all laughed, including Walker—and he took the pen and signed the paper.

Next, the quartet knocked on Eddie Stanky's door.

"C'mon in!" he shouted.

They stepped inside and found their teammate soaking his right elbow in a bucket of ice. "What's going on?" he asked.

Higbe answered. "Got a petition goin' on, Stank."

"To keep Robinson up in Montreal where he belongs," Bragan added.

"Oh." Stanky pondered that. "Did Pee Wee sign it?" he asked finally. Pee Wee Reese was the team captain.

Higbe shook his head. "Ain't asked him yet. What difference does it make?"

Stanky shrugged. "None, just wonderin'." He studied his teammates. Walker couldn't quite meet his eyes. Finally, Stanky

indicated his arm. "Can't sign now. I'm indisposed. Could I catch up with you later?"

After him, they went to Pee Wee's room, but he cut them off before they could get beyond the word *petition*.

"Look, it's like this," he told them bluntly. "I got a wife, a baby, and I got no money. I don't want to step in anything." He directed his next words straight at Walker, as the senior member of the foursome. "Skip me, Dix, I'm not interested."

"What if they put him at shortstop?" Walker demanded.

But Pee Wee just shrugged. "If he's man enough to take my job, I suppose he deserves it."

Higbe snorted. "Not a chance!"

"He does not have the ice water in his veins for big league baseball," Walker argued.

But Reese wouldn't budge. "So let him show what he's got," he answered. "Robinson can play or he can't. It'll all take care of itself."

They had better luck with Pennsylvania-bred Carl Furillo. Despite being the son of immigrants himself, Furillo had no qualms at all. "Give me the pen," he said at once, and signed the second he had it in hand. Higbe grinned. One more to their roster.

Later that night, Durocher's phone rang. He sighed and answered it.

"Yes, Mr. Rickey?" He didn't even have to ask who it was. Who else would call him at this hour?

"Have our friends in the press gone to sleep yet?" Rickey asked.

Durocher peered at the clock. "We are the only people awake on this entire isthmus, Mr. Rickey."

Rickey's voice took on a sharper tone. "A deliberate violation of the law needs a little show of force. I leave it to you. Good night, Leo."

"Yes, Mr. Rickey." Durocher didn't have to ask what his boss was talking about. They'd both heard the chatter earlier today. He knew what some of his players had been up to. And, as he levered himself up out of bed, he vowed that it would stop right now.

Twenty minutes later, Durocher stood in the hotel kitchen in his bathrobe, arms crossed, glaring as his players and coaches filed in. All of them were bleary-eyed, in various states of dress, wondering why he'd gotten them up so early and why he'd gathered them here, of all places.

But Durocher had picked the kitchen for four reasons: It

was big, it was deserted, it was away from prying eyes, and it had things like the soup pot he grabbed now and heaved across the room. *Wham!* That got their attention!

"Wake up, ladies!" he bellowed at them. "Wake up!" He stared down any attempt to talk back. "It's come to my attention that some of you fellas don't want to play with Robinson. That you even got a petition drawn up that you're all gonna sign. Well, boys, you know what you can do with your petition? You can eat it, for all I care!"

It was Walker who found his voice first. "C'mon, Leo . . ." he started.

Durocher hit him with the full force of his glare. "'Come on' what?"

"Ballplayers gotta live together, shower together," Walker argued. "It's not right to force him on us. Besides, I own a hardware store back home, and I—"

"No one cares about your hardware store, Dix!" Durocher cut him off. "And if you don't like it, leave! Mr. Rickey'll be happy to make other arrangements for you."

Studying them all, Durocher suddenly stalked toward Higbe. He'd heard that the pitcher had been the one to start all this. Higbe gulped as the coach approached, but Durocher didn't flatten him, much as he wanted to. Instead, he turned so he could bellow at his whole team, Higbe most of all.

"I don't care if he's yellow or black or has stripes like a zebra," he shouted, his words echoing off the sinks and shelves and stoves. "If Robinson can help us win—and everything I've seen says he can—then he's gonna play for this ball club. Like it, lump it, make your mind up to it, because he's coming! And think about this when your heads hit the pillow—he's only the first, boys, only the first. More are coming right behind him. They have talent and they wanna play!" He let that sink in for a moment. "Yes, sir, they're gonna come diving and scratching. So I'd forget your petition and worry about the field. Because unless you fellas pay a little more attention to your work, they are going to run you right out of the ballpark! A petition?" He glared at them. "Are you ballplayers or lawyers?"

Then he turned and marched past them through the kitchen doors. Behind him, his team muttered and grumbled, but Durocher knew he'd put the fear of God into them. And the fear of Leo Durocher and Branch Rickey. He hoped that would be enough.

Jackie didn't have any trouble getting to practice this year, and when he stepped out onto the field in Panama in his Montreal uniform, he felt confident, in control. But that ended

the second he saw Sukeforth heading toward him, decked out in a Dodgers uniform.

"Robinson!" the talent scout and coach called. Then he tossed something over. Jackie caught it reflexively, then glanced down, recognizing the feel of worn leather. It was a first baseman's glove.

"What do you want me to do with this?" Jackie asked.

Sukeforth raised an eyebrow. "Play first base," he answered, as if that were obvious.

Jackie shook his head. "I've never played first base in my life, Coach."

"Well, it's like this," the coach explained. "Brooklyn's got a solid second baseman. And they got Pee Wee Reese at short. But first base is up for grabs." He broke into a big, warm, friendly smile. "Are you catching my drift?"

Jackie nodded. "Yeah. I don't need a glove to do that."

Sukeforth ambled over to the dugout and grabbed a bucket of baseballs and a bat. Then he returned to home plate and started hitting grounders out to Jackie. At first, Jackie had trouble catching the wicked little hops, and he fumbled his tosses to the little Panamanian kids who had appeared from nowhere and taken up residence at second and third. But after a few rounds, Jackie felt he was starting to get the hang of it.

"Mr. Rickey said he wants you playing conspicuous

baseball!" Sukeforth explained as he hit ball after ball toward Jackie. "To be so good the Dodgers'll demand you on the team! So I thought about it awhile and then I looked up *conspicuous* in the dictionary. It means 'to attract notice or attention.'"

On that last hit, Jackie dove and snagged the ball, then fired it to second, almost knocking the kid off the bag from the force of his throw. That was more like it! He looked over at Sukeforth, who paused and tilted back his cap.

Then the coach grinned and gave him a big thumbs-up. "Conspicuous."

"Bragan," Rickey said, staring at the catcher across his desk at the Tivoli Hotel, "most of your teammates have recanted on this petition nonsense. Are you really here to tell me you don't want to play with Robinson?"

"Yes, sir," Bragan answered. "My friends back in Birmingham would never forgive me."

"And your friends here in Brooklyn?" Rickey asked. But Bragan just shrugged. "Then I will accommodate you." He frowned and sharpened his tone. "If you give me your word that you will try your very best for this team until I can work out a trade."

Apparently, Bragan didn't much like the suggestion that

he might slack off, because he jumped up from his chair and pounded both hands on the desk. "Do you think I would quit on anyone?" he demanded. "I don't quit."

Rickey stared him down, only the edge in his voice showing his anger—or his disgust. "Only on yourself, apparently," he snapped. "You can go, Bragan."

Jackie was getting better and better at playing first base, but he was still the second baseman for Montreal. And second was where he played that afternoon when they practiced against the Dodgers. Dixie Walker was on first when the batter hit the ball straight toward short. Their shortstop snagged it on the hop, then tossed it to Jackie as Walker barreled toward him.

His feet solidly on second, Jackie knew Walker was done. He fired the ball to first, aiming to beat the runner there. He was so focused on that, he didn't even realize that Walker hadn't stopped until the other man slammed into him just as the ball left his hand. They went down together in a tangle, but Jackie didn't care. He glanced up, as did Walker, both of them looking to first—where the Montreal player was standing pretty and grinning. The Dodgers player, on the other hand, was walking away, cursing up a blue streak.

Jackie smiled at that. Beside him, Walker scowled. But so

what? That was the game. Jackie didn't hold it against Walker. The Dodger had tried to rattle him, make him throw wild so the runner could get safely to first even if he himself was already out at second. It hadn't worked, but Jackie didn't fault him for trying. He'd have done the same.

"I received your letter, Dixie," Rickey told Walker as they sat in his office. He lifted it from his desk and read aloud: "'Recently, the thought has occurred to me that a change of ball clubs would benefit both the Brooklyn Baseball Club and myself.'"

Setting the letter down, Rickey asked bluntly, "This is about Robinson?"

But Walker wasn't a hothead like Bragan. "I'm keeping my reasons private," he answered slowly. "Hope you can respect that, sir."

Rickey sighed. "I realize, Dixie, that you have a Southern upbringing, that you would have to subordinate your feelings for the welfare of this venture. I, for one, would deeply appreciate it. I think we can all learn something." He liked Walker, always had—the man was a solid hitter, a good fielder, and a team player. He didn't want to lose him.

But Walker shook his head. "What I have, Mr. Rickey, is

a hardware store back home. It's called Dixie Walker's. Folks don't come because I have the lowest prices, they come because it's called Dixie Walker's. Understand? And I make as much money owning that store as I do playing for you."

Rickey studied him. "Is that what you're afraid of?" Walker didn't respond. "Bragan's a third-stringer," Rickey tried again, "but you bat cleanup. You're popular in Brooklyn. Children look up to you!"

Walker didn't say anything to that. Instead he said simply, "You got my letter. Can I go?"

Rickey sighed, but nodded. "I'll start looking for a trade or a sale. But it won't happen until I get value in return. Until then I expect you to drive in runs."

The other man rose to his feet. "I always have," he replied with quiet dignity. "That's my job."

Rickey watched him go. That was a shame. But if Walker was the only good player he lost over this, he'd count himself lucky. And if he got Robinson in return, he knew he would still come out on top.

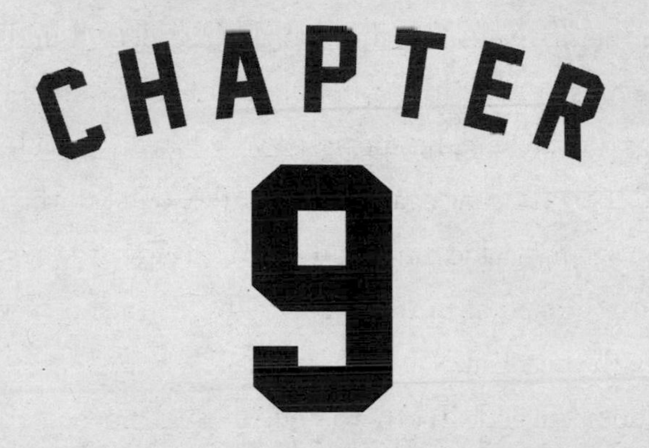

CHAPTER 9

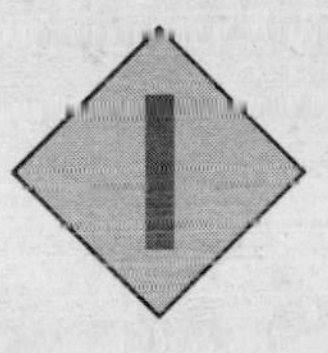

It was late at night on April 8 when Jackie exited Penn Station. He was tired, grumpy, and more than a little confused. Coach Sukeforth had told him that he was wanted up here in New York, that Mr. Rickey wanted to talk to him in person, but hadn't said what it was about. A part of Jackie wondered if he was getting cut, but that didn't make much sense—they could have told him that down in Panama! Coach had refused to say any more, and Jackie had traveled all the way up here worrying over it and trying to puzzle it out, with no success.

Now he stepped out of the station, his suitcases in hand, and looked around. He didn't know New York City at all, wasn't sure where to find a good hotel, but figured he could hail a cab

and ask the driver to take him someplace decent and not too pricey. Yet as he took in the people bustling about and the tall buildings everywhere, he spotted a very familiar Buick.

And there, leaning against it, was Wendell Smith.

"You again," Jackie muttered, stomping toward the reporter.

Smith blinked at him. "That's right, me again. Something wrong with that, Jack?"

Jackie shrugged. Truth to tell, he had no real reason to dislike Smith—the man had only ever been kind and polite to him. But Jackie hated having to rely on somebody else. At least with a cab he'd be paying the driver, so he wasn't getting help, he was getting service. But Smith giving him a ride? That was different.

He didn't say any of that, however. He'd never been much of a talker, except sometimes with Rae. Instead he just grumbled, "Come on," and stepped around Smith to toss his luggage into the backseat.

"Yes, suh!" Smith replied. He saluted Jackie, and the pair took off.

As they drove through the Manhattan traffic—heavy even at this late hour—Jackie could feel Smith glancing over at him every so often. Finally, the reporter spoke:

"They can't keep you on Montreal for long. After these exhibition games, they've got to bring you up." He let that hang in the air for a second, but Jackie didn't much feel like talking. "You don't have two words to rub together, do you?"

"Do I have to entertain you?" Jackie snapped. He regretted it immediately, but he wasn't about to admit that. Instead he folded his arms over his chest and glared out the window.

Next to him, Smith sighed. "You ever wonder why I sit out in right field with my typewriter on my knees?" he asked. "Does that ever cross your mind?"

Jackie just stared at the skyscrapers as they slid past.

That didn't slow Smith down one bit, though. "It's because Negro reporters aren't allowed in the press box."

That hadn't occurred to Jackie, and now he felt horrible for never asking. Of course Smith had to type on his lap. Why hadn't he realized that? And now he was too embarrassed to apologize.

After a few minutes, Smith shook his head. Then, in a deep, gravelly voice Jackie guessed was supposed to be him, Smith declared, "You know, Wendell, I never asked you where you were from?"

"Why, I'm from Detroit, Jack," Smith answered in his own voice.

He switched back to his Jackie impersonation. "You don't say? Tell me more."

Jackie shook his head and tried to block it all out, all the chatter, but he could still hear Smith's explanation loud and clear:

"My daddy used to work at Fair Lane. That was Mr. Ford's estate. My daddy was Mr. Henry Ford's cook."

As "Jackie," he frowned. "I did not know that."

"Oh, yes." Smith nodded. "Cooked for him for years, but never once broke bread with him. I'd go to work with Daddy sometimes. Play baseball out on the lawn with Mr. Ford's grandchildren. We all had a real good time. But it was understood, if they got tired of playing ball and moved inside to the bowling alley or swimming pool, I was not invited or allowed. The grass was as far as I got. So, guess what? You're not the only one with something at stake here."

Jackie thought about that. "If I start talking, will you stop?" he asked.

Smith laughed. "I'd be happy to."

He stopped at a red light, and Jackie turned to face him more fully. "I apologize," he told Smith. "You've supported me through this more than anyone besides Rae and Mr. Rickey. But I guess that's what bothers me."

He could hear the other man's uncertainty, so like his own. "How do you mean?"

Jackie braced himself for the truth. "I don't like needing help. I don't like needing anyone but myself. I never have."

Smith sighed. "You are a hard case, Jack Robinson. Is it okay if I keep driving you, or should I let you out so you can walk?"

Startled, Jackie glanced around, taking in the hordes of people still up at this hour, running this way and that. He had absolutely no idea where anything outside this car was, how to get anywhere, whom to ask for directions.

Finally, he started laughing. After a minute, so did Smith. They both sat there for a minute chuckling, the tension between them finally swept away.

"Hey," Jackie said suddenly. "You remember the last time we were at a red light? Down in Florida?"

Smith laughed. "New York City now, baby. We've come a long way."

Jackie just nodded and craned his neck to peer up at the stars and the tall, gleaming buildings shutting them out. "And we got a long way to go."

Smith smiled and gave the Buick a little more gas, and they shot off into the night.

The next morning, Rickey sat in his office, clutching that morning's edition of the *New York Sun*. Parrott listened as Rickey read aloud from an article that had incensed him.

"'Branch Rickey cannot afford to upset team chemistry,

and so the only thing keeping Robinson off the Dodgers now, plainly, is the attitude of the players. If it softens at the sight of Jackie's skills, he'll join the club sometime between April tenth and April fifteenth. Otherwise, Robinson will spend the year back in Montreal.'"

Rickey hurled the paper down onto his desk. "For the love of Pete," he shouted. "He batted six twenty-five in the exhibition games against them . . . us . . . them—against us! Judas Priest!"

In the outer office, he heard the phone ring, but he ignored it. His secretary, Jane Ann, would handle it. That was what he paid her for, after all.

"Maybe you could have Durocher hold a press conference," Parrott suggested. "Demand that he get Robinson on his team."

Rickey calmed down a little. "Durocher. Of course; he's my ace in the hole. Very good, Harold." He knew there'd been a reason he'd stolen Harold away from the newspapers to be the Dodgers' traveling secretary. He was a good man, and a sharp one. And he was right. Durocher could handle this for them.

The phone was still ringing, Rickey realized, and he glanced toward his door. "Jane Ann!" he called. "Are you out there?" No one answered—perhaps she'd taken a bathroom break or run out to get a coffee. Well, the ringing was driving him mad, so there was nothing for it—Rickey leaned over and grabbed up the phone on his desk. "Branch Rickey," he announced into

the receiver. "You're speaking to him . . . the commissioner of what? Oh, yes, put him on." He dropped back into his chair and looked over at Parrott. "The commissioner of baseball."

"Branch, how are you?" Rickey could almost see Happy Chandler through the phone—the commissioner was a big, cheerful man with a large, flat head, hair carefully parted in the middle, and an ever-present jovial smile. But behind that smile he was all business, and Rickey could already guess he wasn't calling with good news.

Still, it was important to mind his manners, so he answered, "Fine. What can I do for you, Happy?"

"Branch," Happy said, as casually as if he were calling to talk about the weather, "how would you feel about losing Durocher for a year?"

What? Rickey frowned and switched the phone from one ear to the other. "I'm sorry, Happy, I thought you said 'lose Durocher for a year.'"

"I did," the commissioner replied. "He was seen in Havana with known gamblers."

Rickey laughed. "Anyone who sets foot in Havana is seen with known gamblers." Which was true, though he knew Durocher was worse about it than most. He was a great coach, but he did like his card games. Among other amusements.

"It's not just one thing," Happy explained, "it's an

accumulation. I received notice today from the Catholic Youth Organization, vowing a ban on baseball unless Durocher is punished for his moral looseness."

"You're joking." But Rickey could tell he wasn't. And he had a bad feeling he knew where this was going.

Sure enough, Happy continued, "It's this business with the actress in California. She's recently divorced and Durocher is the cause. They may even be illegally married."

Rickey shook his head. "Now I'm sure you're joking." What was Durocher thinking? He'd tried to warn the man about seeing that actress, but did Leo listen? Of course not!

"I wish I were," Happy said. He sounded as insincere as ever, though. Rickey knew that the commissioner had never been one of Durocher's biggest fans. It didn't help that Happy was a good friend of Larry MacPhail, the new Yankees owner—and that MacPhail and Durocher had been trading insults ever since the Yankees had stolen away two of their coaches. Leo had some pretty choice words for MacPhail, and now it looked like MacPhail may have called on his buddy to help him even the score. Though it apparently wasn't just about that feud, as Happy was quick to point out. "The CYO buy a lot of tickets, Branch. They draw a lot of water, and I can't afford to ruffle their feathers. Am I mixing metaphors there?"

Rickey sighed. "You know very well my organization

is about to enter a tempest," he admitted to Happy. "I need Durocher at the rudder. He's the only man who can handle this much trouble—who loves it, in fact. You're chopping off my right hand!"

But his plea fell on deaf ears. "I have no choice," Happy claimed. "I'm going to have to sit your manager, Branch. Leo Durocher is suspended from baseball for a year."

"You can't do that!" Rickey hollered into the phone, finally losing his temper. "Happy, you—" But he was talking to a dial tone. Rickey steadied himself, then glanced up at Parrott. "Trouble ahead, Harold," he told his employee. "Trouble."

Still, Rickey wasn't about to let losing Durocher derail his plans. That was why, the following morning, the ring of a phone woke Jackie in his hotel room.

"Hello?" he said after grasping for the receiver and getting it somewhere near his mouth.

"Mr. Robinson," a woman replied, sounding far too awake for this early in the morning. "It's Jane Ann, in Mr. Rickey's office. He needs to see you right away. He has a contract for you to sign."

That woke Jackie up in a hurry!

An hour later, he was sitting in Rickey's office, which

looked the same as it had three years before. Even the goldfish were still there. He was staring at them when Rickey entered, carrying a contract in his hands. He set it down on the desk in front of Jackie and handed him a pen.

"I'm so sorry about the rush," Rickey told him. "Events are unfolding too fast to keep up with. The burden has finally fallen to me, and so be it."

Jackie didn't know what Rickey was talking about, exactly—and he didn't much care. All that mattered to him right now was the piece of paper in front of him, and the fact that it put together two very important names: "Jack Roosevelt Robinson" and "Brooklyn Dodgers." He barely glanced at the rest before pointing near the bottom. "Sign here?"

Rickey nodded. "Yes, yes." But as Jackie started lowering the pen to the page, the Dodgers general manager suddenly shouted, "Stop!"

Jackie froze.

"History," Rickey announced out of nowhere. "And I'm blabbing, blabbing through history, rushing it along. What am I thinking?" He stuck his head out the door. "Jane Ann, come in here," he called, then twisted to holler farther down the hall. "Harold!" Parrott stuck his head out from an office down the hall. "Gather some of our employees and get them up here!"

A few minutes later, Jackie was finally allowed to sign

the contract. As he set the pen down, Rickey started clapping. So did Parrott, Jane Ann, and a janitor—the only employee Parrott had been able to find in the building this early.

"Excellent!" Rickey clapped Jackie on the shoulder. "Harold, telegram the press. Say this: 'The Brooklyn Dodgers today purchased the contract of Jackie Robinson from the Montreal Royals. He will report immediately.'"

Parrott hurried off, Jane Ann returned to her desk, and the janitor went back to mopping floors. And Jackie sat there, still trying to take it all in.

The sun was just rising in Pasadena when the phone rang at the Isum house. Rachel answered it, already awake but still in her nightgown. "Hello?"

"Rae," Jackie said over the phone, "I'm in Brooklyn." The glee in his voice was clear.

Brooklyn! Rachel let out a whoop, then quieted, guiltily glancing down the hall to where Jackie Junior had just settled back to sleep. She waited a second but didn't hear any crying. She hadn't woken him again. Whew! She kept her voice quiet as she turned her attention back to her husband. Which was fine, since all she had to say was, "What did I tell you?"

Jackie's laugh was music to her ears.

CHAPTER 10

ough syrup, tissues, cotton balls . . ." Jackie walked slowly down the aisle of Singer's Drug Store, scanning the products on each side. At last he spotted the small pink bottle he'd been looking for. "Ah, there you are!" He claimed some Pepto-Bismol off the shelf just as someone in the next aisle over took a bottle from that side, and Jackie glanced up—to find himself staring into the face of Pee Wee Reese.

"Opening-day nerves," Reese commented as they left the store together, hefting the bottle in his hand. "Doing my stomach something awful."

Jackie nodded. He was having the same problem, which was why he'd come here. The first game of the season—his first

game in the major leagues—was starting soon, and his stomach was tied completely in knots.

As they stood there, neither one saying anything, a garbage truck rumbled past, its odor wafting along ahead of it and lingering behind.

Reese chuckled. "There goes another one," he said, gesturing toward the truck. "Every time I see a garbage truck go by, I still can't figure why the guy driving isn't me."

Jackie smiled at that. He didn't know the Dodgers shortstop well, but so far he liked the man. "We'd both better get on base."

Reese nodded, and they started walking toward the stadium together. "Know when I first heard of you?" he said after a minute.

Jackie shook his head.

"On a troop transport, coming back from Guam," Reese told him. "A sailor heard it on the radio, told me the Dodgers had signed a Negro player. I said that was fine by me. Then he said the guy was a shortstop. Least you were then. That got me thinking. Thinking gets me scared."

Jackie smiled and lifted his bottle of Pepto in mock salute. "Black, white—we're both pink today, huh?"

Reese nodded.

They walked a few more blocks before Jackie broke the

silence by asking the question he couldn't get out of his mind: "You still scared, Pee Wee?"

His teammate looked around. And then he smiled. "Of garbage trucks?" he answered. "Terrified."

And both of them laughed.

They reached Ebbets Field, and as they entered the Dodgers locker room, everyone there stopped to look at Jackie. He did his best to ignore them as he searched for his locker.

Not every face was unfriendly, though. Two players came right over to him.

"I'm Hermanski," one of them offered, along with his hand. "Welcome to Brooklyn."

"Hey, man," the other said, also shaking with Jackie. "Ralph Branca." Jackie remembered Branca waving at him, that time down in Daytona Beach.

Then a familiar face joined them and slapped Jackie on the back. It was Spider Jorgensen, who had been on the Royals with him.

"We made it, huh, Jack, huh?" Jorgensen told him. "Good luck."

"You, too, man," Jackie said, thumping him back. He'd

Branch Rickey had to convince his staff to add a talented black player to the Brooklyn Dodgers roster

He found one in Jackie Robinson who had been playing with the Kansas City Monarchs in the Negro Leagues.

Jackie discussed how joining the white baseball league would affect him with his wife, Rachel.

Meanwhile, Rickey continued to gather support, from the farm team Jackie started with up to the major-league Dodgers.

Not every member of Rickey's own team wanted Jackie around. A few players started a petition to get rid of him

But Dodgers manager Leo Durocher set them straight.

Jackie Robinson was a Dodger, whether anyone liked it or not.

Jackie learned that all of his teammates had things on their minds before a big game.

But while white players only worried about playing ball, Jackie had other things on his mind.

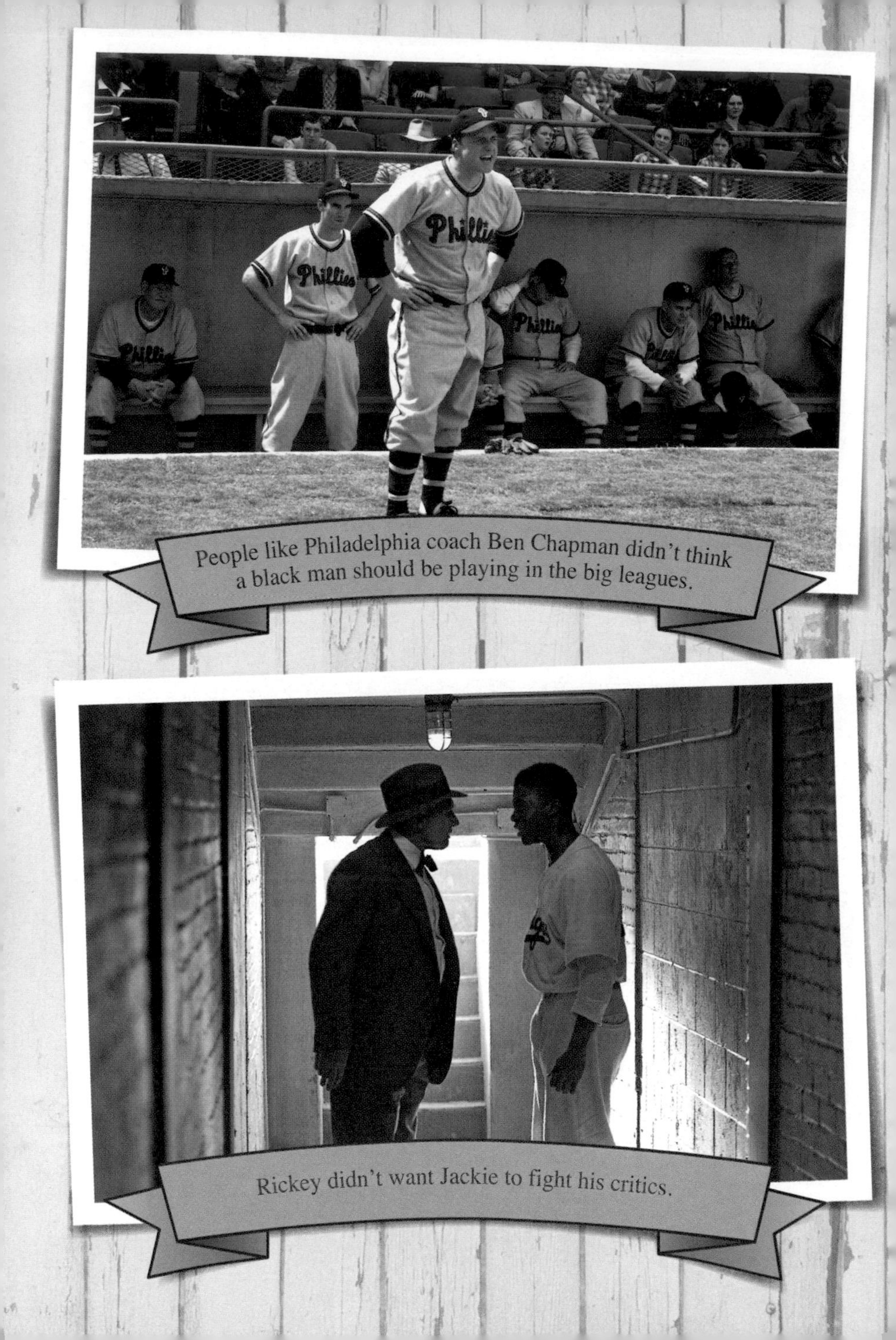

People like Philadelphia coach Ben Chapman didn't think a black man should be playing in the big leagues.

Rickey didn't want Jackie to fight his critics.

He wanted Jackie to prove them wrong
by playing good ball.

Rickey and Rachel both believed in Jackie.

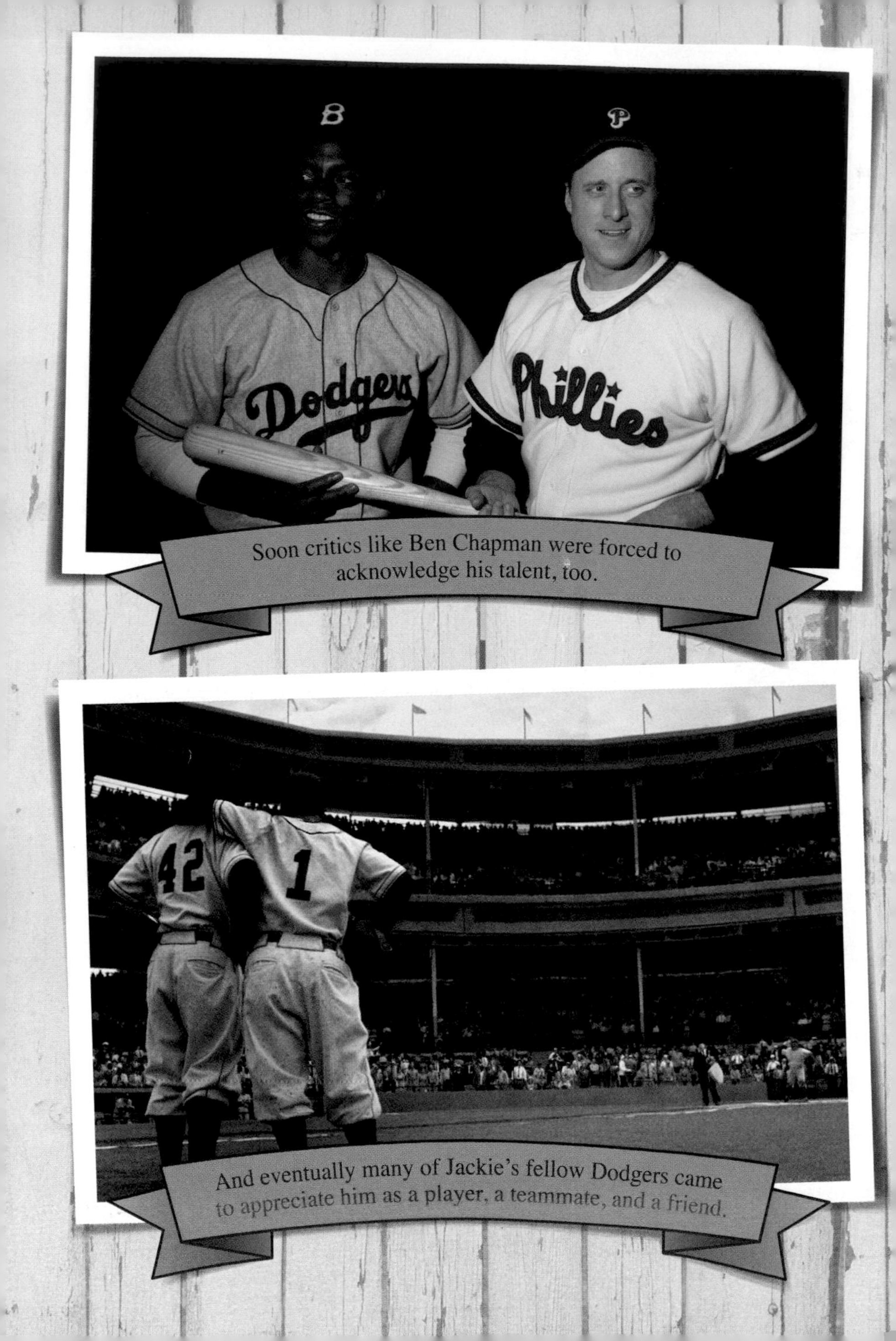
Dodgers
Phillies
Soon critics like Ben Chapman were forced to acknowledge his talent, too.
42
1
And eventually many of Jackie's fellow Dodgers came to appreciate him as a player, a teammate, and a friend.

always gotten along with Jorgensen, right from that first day of spring training.

As the others drifted away to get ready, Jackie continued looking for his locker. He was starting to get concerned, and maybe a little annoyed, when an older guy came over to him.

"You're looking for your locker, kid?" he asked, and Jackie guessed he was Babe Hamburger, the clubhouse manager. "Follow me."

Hamburger led Jackie over to the corner, where there was a uniform hanging from an exposed hook. A folding chair had been placed below that.

"I just got the word," Hamburger explained. "Best I could do. I'll get you straightened out tomorrow though, huh?"

Jackie stared at him for a second, wondering if this was a prank, but the older man looked genuinely sorry, and it *had* been short notice. So he just nodded and started unbuttoning his shirt. What did it matter if he didn't have a regular locker yet, he decided. He was a Dodger, his uniform was here, and he was going to play. That was all he needed.

He'd just started getting ready, however, when Jackie felt somebody else standing in his space. He glanced up to see a little guy in a Dodger uniform glaring at him. He recognized the player as Eddie Stanky, the second baseman.

"You putting on that uniform," Stanky told Jackie sharply, getting in his face, "means you're on my team. But before I play with you I want you to know how I feel about it. I want you to know I don't like it. I want you to know I don't like you."

Jackie stared at him for a minute. He had more than a few inches over Stanky, and at least twenty pounds, but the little guy didn't flinch or back away. And he wasn't spitting curses or insults. Jackie had to give him credit for that.

"That's fine," he told Stanky. "That's how I prefer it. Right out in the open."

Stanky nodded back and walked away, and Jackie went back to suiting up. If that was the worst he'd get on this team, he was doing pretty well.

"C'mon, Brooklyn!" a hot-dog vendor shouted from behind his stand. "Get your Harry M. Stevens special here!" He handed one over to a customer, accepting a pair of dimes in return. Then he turned and searched for someone in the seats nearby. "Hey, lady!" Rachel looked over, baby Jackie in her arms, as the grizzled old vendor took a baby bottle out of the hot water in his steamer and offered it to her with a smile. "I think it's ready."

Rachel smiled and thanked him, and turned to get her son situated. There was a commotion on the field, and she glanced up to see the Dodgers making their way out of the tunnel from their locker room. And there, number forty-two, was her man. A cheer broke out all around her as he came into view, and Rachel held Jackie Junior up so he could see his father. "There's Daddy," she whispered to him. "That's who they're all cheering for, you know." Jackie was looking around, scanning the stands, and finally their eyes met. He smiled and waved, and Rachel felt her heart burst with pride. He looked so fine in his Dodgers uniform!

After a moment, she took her seat and watched as they sang the national anthem. And then it was time to play some ball!

The cheers continued when number forty-two, Jackie Robinson, finally stepped up to the plate for the first time. Overhead, he could hear the local sportscaster, Red Barber, announcing, "One out in the bottom of the first. Headed toward the plate for his first big-league at bat is Dodger rookie Jackie Robinson. Jackie is very definitely brunette." That got a few laughs and a lot more cheers, and Jackie smiled.

He settled into his stance at home plate, bat raised high, and studied the Boston Braves pitcher, Johnny Sain. "Sain looking in," he heard Barber report. "When he's got that fastball working, he can toss a lamb chop past a hungry wolf."

Sain threw him a fastball—and Jackie slammed it down the third base line. *Crack!*

The Braves' third baseman snagged the ball after its first bounce, but Jackie was already flying toward first. His foot hit the bag right before the ball smacked into the first baseman's mitt. He was happily slowing down and struggling to catch his breath when he heard the umpire clearly say, "You're out!"

What? Jackie glared at him, but the umpire stared back, daring him to complain. Jackie just shook his head, fighting back his anger. He'd been safe and he knew it. But what could he do? It was a bad call, and that sort of thing happened to everybody, no matter what color. But did it have to be on his very first at bat in the majors?

"It's a game of inches, Jackie!" a voice called down, and Jackie glanced up to see Rickey smiling at him from a seat just above the dugout. The general manager didn't look upset at all—at least, not at Jackie.

Next to him, however, Parrott was hollering toward the field, "Get some glasses, ump!"

A few days later, Rickey sat waiting in his office as he listened to footsteps and voices coming down the hall.

"How's Florida, Burt?" he heard Parrott ask.

"Roses need pruning," Burt Shotton answered, "but it was fine when I left it last night. Branch said it was important and I heard about Leo. Any idea what this is about?"

Rickey held his breath, but all Parrott said was, "You'd better just talk to him." *Good man!*

There was a knock at the door, and Rickey straightened his glasses. "Come in!" He smiled at the two men as they entered, but directed his words toward Shotton. "Baseball has returned to Brooklyn, Burt. Another season is underway."

Shotton nodded. "Yeah, it's a shame about Leo."

Rickey leaned back in his chair. "Inevitable, I suppose. I asked him if she was worth it and he said yes. How's the retirement?" Shotton had been an outfielder for the Cardinals back in the day, and had started filling in as temporary manager back in the twenties, covering Sundays only. Rickey had been the coach then, and he'd needed Sundays so he could attend church. Shotton had become the Cardinals coach himself in 1923, and had then coached the Phillies, the Reds, and several farm clubs before retiring in 1946. But Rickey wasn't ready to let him go just yet.

"It's fine," Shotton started. "The roses—"

"It's a wonderful thing when a man has good health and enough money and absolutely nothing to do," Rickey commented.

Shotton rose to the bait. "I'm perfectly happy."

"Is that so?" Rickey shot back.

His old friend peered down at him. "When I took off that Cleveland uniform two years ago, I promised the missus I'd never put on another uniform again. Roses look great and I sleep a whole lot better."

"Roses and sleep are two wonderful things, Burt," Rickey agreed. "But sleep you can get inside your casket and flowers look good on top of it. You don't look like a dead man to me."

Shotton sighed. "What's this about, Branch?" All the telegram had said was "Be in Brooklyn in the morning. Call nobody, see no one." A little dramatic, maybe, but clearly it had worked.

Now, however, Rickey saw no reason to beat around the bush. "I want you to manage the Dodgers," he told Shotton. "We're a ship without a captain, and there's a typhoon ahead."

But Shotton shook his head. "No. I'm sorry, but no."

Rickey studied him. "Do you miss the game, Burt? Look me in the eye and tell me you don't."

Shotton considered Rickey's words for a second—though he couldn't meet his gaze—but still shook his head. "Baseball's the only life for an old pepper pot like me, but I promised my wife, Branch."

"You promised her you wouldn't put on another uniform," Rickey corrected with a smile. "You didn't promise her you wouldn't manage. Wear a suit and tie—Connie Mack still does." Shotton didn't reply, so Rickey pressed his advantage. "You remember how to get to the Polo Grounds, Burt?" That was where the Dodgers had their practices.

"Branch, I—" Shotton started, but Rickey cut him off.

"You remember what the peanuts smell like roasting, how the crack of the bat sounds, the roar of the crowd?" Rickey knew he wasn't being entirely fair, but he was desperate. The Dodgers needed a coach, and he needed it to be someone he could trust.

Finally, Shotton nodded. "Sure."

Rickey tossed him a set of car keys. "My car's parked right out front. Harold will show you where. Now, what do you say?"

And, just as he'd hoped, his old friend nodded. "Okay." And Rickey knew Shotton wasn't just talking about getting to go see the Dodgers play.

X X X

That afternoon, Shotton addressed the Dodgers in the locker room.

"Men," he announced, "I don't have much to say. Just—don't be afraid of old Burt Shotton as a manager. You can win the pennant in spite of me. I cannot possibly hurt you."

The players looked at one another, Jackie right along with the rest. What kind of a speech was that? Was that just the way

Shotton talked? He was certainly calm and laid-back, not like Durocher with his temper. But was this a good thing or a bad thing?

As Shotton turned to go, he spotted Jackie, who was right in his path.

"Are you Robinson?" he asked as he approached. Jackie nodded. "I thought so." Shotton patted him on the shoulder, then continued on his way. Jackie wasn't sure what to make of that, either, but at least the new coach didn't seem to have a problem with him being there.

"Mark my words," Rickey overheard *Herald Tribune* reporter Bob Cooke say that afternoon. The reporters were all in the press box, of course, watching the game and getting ready to tell their listeners and readers all about it. "Mark my words and circle this date. Negroes are going to run the white man straight out of baseball. I'm not prejudiced; it's physiological. They have a longer heel bone. Gives 'em an unfair speed advantage."

The reason for this speech, of course, was that Jackie had just been announced. Rickey peered down at the field and saw Jackie standing at the plate, his bat cocked and ready.

"Here's Robinson," Barber reported. "Jackie holds that club down by the end. Rear foot on the back line of the box.

Slight open stance, bent at the knees—" Just then the Giants pitcher, Dave Koslo, went into his windup and released. Jackie swung—*crack!* The ball went soaring out over left field. A home run! The crowd went crazy as Jackie started his way around the bases.

In the press box, Rickey heard the sound of rapid typing. Then one of the reporters called out, "Was that because his heels are longer, Bob?" The press box erupted with laughter. Rickey turned away, smiling, and made his way back to his own seat. Things were starting to shape up nicely.

"I'm not complaining," Jackie told Rachel. "I just—I don't know what they want."

He had taken her out to dinner, something they didn't get to do nearly often enough. Jackie loved his son, of course, but it was nice to have an evening out, just the two of them. It was a good thing they'd found Alice, their new babysitter! They were at Lawson Bowman's Café, a classy new steakhouse and nightclub. But Jackie hadn't gotten a chance to even try his steak yet. Every time he tried to take a bite, someone asked him for his autograph, or took his picture, or just came over to shake his hand and tell him how happy they were to see him on the Dodgers. It was the strangest thing.

Rachel apparently didn't think so. "They want to see if Jackie Robinson is real," she told him happily. "They want to see your pride, your dignity. Because then they'll see it in themselves."

Jackie stared at her. Would he ever stop being astounded by how smart she was, how insightful? And how lovely?

"And me?" she added, almost shyly. "I'm just young and scared and amazed at how brave you are."

He grinned at her, and raised his fork to his mouth—but just before it got there, a man appeared beside him, pulled up a chair, and dropped into it. He had his hand out already, and Jackie shook it automatically.

"I'm Lawson Bowman, Jack," the man told him proudly. "The owner of this joint. How's the steak?"

Jackie shook his head. "I'm not sure yet," he replied. "It looks good."

Rachel laughed at that, and so did Bowman. And Jackie couldn't help joining in.

CHAPTER 11

achel waited anxiously, Jackie Junior in her arms, her eyes on the clock. Where was Alice? Just then, there was a knock at the door.

"Sorry I'm late," the young woman said breathlessly as Rachel ushered her inside. "Class ran long."

Rachel smiled. "It's okay." She could hardly be mad about that, and besides, she liked Alice. She handed the baby over. "It's so cold and raw out, I don't want him getting sick at the game," she explained.

"He'll be nice and warm here," the babysitter promised. Jackie Junior cooed—he liked Alice, too.

Rachel kissed him one last time, glanced at her watch, frowned, and headed out the door. She was going to be a little late, but she tried not to miss any of Jackie's games. And this was the first game against the Phillies this season. It was a big one.

Jackie stepped up to bat in the bottom of the first. Stanky was already safe on first base. But just as Jackie reached the plate, he heard a voice behind him shout, "Hey! Hey, you black nigger!"

Jackie glanced up to see a man standing at the top of the visitors' dugout. He wore the Phillies uniform, and with a start Jackie realized that it was the team manager himself, Ben Chapman.

"Why don't you go back to the cotton fields where you belong?!" Chapman hollered. Jackie stared at him. He'd gotten insults before, of course, but this was the manager! Wasn't he supposed to be the one keeping his players in line? "Or did you swing your way out of the jungle?" Chapman continued. "Bring me a banana!" He started hooting and making monkey faces.

"The Phillies manager Ben Chapman is up on the top step," Barber announced over the speakers. "He seems to be chirping something out to Robinson. Of course, Chapman was a hot-head during his playing days with the Yankees."

Rickey leaned forward in his seat next to Parrott. "What's

he saying?" But Parrott shook his head. They weren't close enough to hear.

Now two of the Phillies players stepped up beside their manager. But if Jackie had hoped they'd make him behave, he was dead wrong.

"Go home, nigger!" the first one yelled.

The second one added, "Go back to Africa!"

Jackie knew better than to respond, so he turned his attention toward the mound. Philly pitcher Dutch Leonard looked in, then threw a fastball, well inside. Jackie had to dive out of the way to avoid getting hit.

"Bojangles!" he heard Chapman shout. "You sure can dance, snowflake!"

Jackie saw Stanky standing on first, his mouth open. It was nice to know that even the prickly second baseman was shocked by Chapman's behavior. There was nothing Jackie could do about it, though, so he focused on the ball again. Play the game, he reminded himself. Not *their* game.

It was another inside fastball, and again he had to jump back out of the way. He glared at the pitcher, who glared right back.

"Ball two!" the umpire called.

"Hey, black boy!" Chapman taunted. "Hey, shoe shine!"

Jackie didn't want to look over, but something made him. The two Phillies players looked angry, which he was used to.

But not Chapman. He was grinning ear to ear. He was enjoying this!

Jackie didn't need to look to guess how his teammates were reacting. Their fury just made Chapman grin wider, though. "Oh, I think I got it," he crowed. "Dixie, I believe I know!"

Jackie tried to tune him out again, watching Leonard and gripping his bat so tight his hands ached. He connected this time, but sent the ball arcing lazily out into left. He was only halfway to first when the left fielder picked it off. At least now he could go back to the dugout and escape Chapman's ugly words.

No one stopped him as he entered. None of his teammates said anything to him. Bobby Bragan glanced over, but then looked away. A minute later they took the field, and Jackie refused to turn toward the visitors' dugout. He did catch sight of Rachel up in the stands, though. She looked horrified and outraged on his behalf. He nodded, but he couldn't smile and wave it off. Not this time.

In the bottom of the third, he got back on deck. Stanky was on first, Jorgensen on second. And just as Jackie stepped up, Chapman rose to his feet again, his two flunkies right beside him.

"Hey, nigger lips!" the first one called.

"Party's over, jungle bunny!" the second added.

"Hey, Pee Wee! Dixie!" Chapman hollered at the other Dodgers. "What's this nigger doing for you all to let him drink from the same water fountain as you? I hope it's worth it!"

Jackie waited on the pitch. When it came, he swung hard—*crack!* But the ball popped up, not even getting as far as the pitcher's mound. The Phillies catcher, Seminick, moved under it and waited.

"Hey, is that a home run?" Leonard asked no one in particular.

The catcher laughed as the ball plopped into his glove. "Yeah—if you're playing in an elevator shaft!"

As Jackie headed back to the dugout, Chapman started in on him again.

"You don't belong!" he hollered. "Look in a mirror! This is a white man's game. Get it through your thick monkey skull!"

That was it. Jackie stopped short and turned, slowly, to glare at Chapman. The manager stood his ground.

Jackie wanted nothing more than to beat that smug look off the man's face. But he remembered what Rickey had said, and what he'd promised. He couldn't fight. He couldn't sink to their level.

Instead he turned and walked away.

He headed down into the dugout, and then beyond that

into the tunnel toward the locker room. Before he reached the locker room, however, he finally exploded. Twisting around, he began beating his bat against the wall. *Wham! Wham!* His bat splintered and shattered, the polished wood unable to withstand his fury. But it wasn't enough. Jackie dropped the bat and pounded his fists together. He wanted to break something, to destroy something, to tear it apart. Something—or someone.

Footsteps echoed down the tunnel. Breathing heavily, hands still clenched, he turned and saw Rickey approaching. The general manager stopped when he saw the devastation. Jackie thought he saw fear in the older man's eyes.

"I'm done with this," Jackie snarled at him. "The next white idiot who opens his mouth, I'll smash his teeth in."

Rickey didn't say anything for a minute. When he did, he didn't sound angry. Just disappointed. "You can't, Jackie. You know it."

Jackie glared at him. "I'm supposed to let this go on?"

"These men have to live with themselves—" Rickey started, but Jackie cut him off.

"I have to live with myself, too! And right now I'm living a sermon out there. I'm through with it!" He kicked bits of bat away from him.

But Rickey wasn't giving up. "You don't matter right now, Jackie," he warned, his voice serious. "You're in this thing. You

don't have the right to pull out from the backing of people who believe in you, respect you, and need you."

"Is that so?" Jackie demanded.

Rickey nodded. "If you fight, they won't say Chapman forced you to; they'll just say that you're in over your head. That you don't belong where you are. That every downtrodden man who wants more from life is in over his head."

Jackie took a step toward him. "Do you know what it's like, having someone do this to you?"

"No," Rickey admitted. "You do. You're the one living the sermon. In the wilderness. Forty days. All of it. Only you."

"And not a thing I can do about it," Jackie said, though it came out as a grumble, almost a whine. He knew how childish he sounded.

"Of course there is!" Rickey assured him. "You can stand up and hit! You can get on base, and you can score! You can win this game for us! We need you! Everyone needs you. You're medicine, Jack." He leaned against the wall, panting as if he'd been the one to slam a bat into the wall over and over again. Jackie just watched him for a minute.

Then he heard other sounds from back on the field. Sounds he recognized.

"They're taking the field," he said aloud.

Rickey smiled. "Who's playing first?"

Jackie thought about that for a minute. Who would cover first base if he didn't go out there, and would they do as good a job as he could? How much was he prepared to take to keep what he'd already won, and to try to build something more? To be the example Rickey was making him into?

Finally, he nodded. "I'm gonna need a new bat." Then he turned and headed back toward the field.

His next at bat didn't come around until the bottom of the eighth. It was still a scoreless game.

As expected, just as he got close to home plate Chapman started in again. "Hey, black nigger! I know you can hear me! If you were a white boy, you know where you'd be right now? On a bus headed down to Newport News, 'cause you can't play at all!"

Really? Jackie knew one thing he did well—very well. When the pitch came, he sent the ball looping out past second. A single, nothing more, but at least now he was standing on first. He didn't expect to be there very long.

Pete Reiser stepped into the batter's box, but Leonard wasn't even watching him. All his attention was focused on Jackie.

And Jackie stared right back as he deliberately took a huge lead off first.

Leonard didn't even hesitate. He fired toward first. The ball was fast, all right, but Jackie was faster. After being declared safe, he stood again. He didn't bother to brush the dirt from his uniform.

Finally, Leonard gave Reiser his attention. And the instant he pitched, Jackie took off toward second. Reiser swung and missed, and the Phillies catcher immediately lobbed the ball to second, but his aim was off and the ball went wide. Jackie put on a burst of speed and rounded the corner to third.

"Look," the Phillies third baseman said to him after Jackie had stopped there, "I'm sorry. I want you to know; what goes on here, it don't go for me."

Jackie nodded ever so slightly. He didn't want to lose his anger right now, but it was nice to know that not every Philly player was like Chapman.

He got ready to run again but wound up not having to—Reiser struck out, but Hermanski cracked a single to left and Jackie was able to trot home, barely breathing hard. He glared at Chapman as he passed, but the Phillies manager spat on the ground, clearly unmoved. Still, he didn't look happy.

"You fellas are making too big a deal out of this," Chapman declared in the visitors' locker room a short while later. "He

scored. We lost. One to nothing." He took a sip of his drink.

"Do you think you were a little hard on Robinson?" one of the reporters asked.

Chapman shook his head. "We treat him the same way we do Hank Greenberg," he claimed, "except we call Hank a kike instead of a coon. When we play exhibitions against the Yankees, we call DiMaggio the Wop. They laugh at it. No harm, it's forgotten after the game ends." He tossed his empty beer can aside.

"Don't you think this was maybe one foot over the line?" a different reporter insisted.

Chapman barked out a laugh. "Hey, let's get the chips off our shoulders and play ball," he said easily. "It's a game, right?"

* * *

Rickey was lost in thought when Parrott walked into his office. "I'm going in that Philly dugout tomorrow," the young traveling secretary charged, "and wringing Chapman's neck!" Rickey surprised him by bursting out laughing. "Did I say something funny?"

Rickey took off his glasses and wiped at his eyes. "When I first told you about Jackie," he pointed out, "you were against it. Now all of a sudden you're worrying about him. How do you suppose that happened?"

Parrott studied his feet. "Well, any decent-minded person—"

His boss cut him off. "*Sympathy,* Harold, is a Greek word. It means 'to suffer.' 'I sympathize with you' means 'I suffer with you.' This Philadelphia manager has done me a service."

"A service?" Parrott stared at him.

His tone made Rickey laugh again. "Is there an echo in here? Yes, he's creating sympathy on Jackie's behalf. *Philadelphia,* by the way, is Greek for 'brotherly love.'"

The buzz of the intercom interrupted him. "Bob Bragan to see you, Mr. Rickey," Jane Ann warned.

That made Rickey's good mood sour. "What does he want?" He stabbed a button on the intercom. "Send him in."

He straightened some papers on his desk and pretended to be busy as Bragan entered.

"What do you want, Bragan?" Rickey barely looked up.

"I'd like not to be traded, sir, if it isn't too late," Bragan answered.

Now Rickey was paying attention. "What about Robinson?"

Bragan had been staring at the floor, but now he looked up and met Rickey's eyes. "I'd like to be his teammate."

Rickey frowned. "Why?"

Bragan shrugged and looked away again. "The world's changing," he said. "I guess I can live with the change."

Rickey considered him for a second. "Well," he drawled, "the Red Sox just offered Ted Williams, but I'll see what I can do." That wasn't even remotely true, of course—Williams was ten times the player Bragan was, and they both knew it.

Bragan nodded. "Thank you, Mr. Rickey."

After he left, Rickey and Parrott just looked at each other. They were both stunned. One of the men behind the petition to keep Jackie from playing now wanted to be Jackie's teammate? What an amazing thing!

Jackie finally stepped out from under the stands and was shocked to find Rachel there. "You shouldn't have waited," he told her.

She graced him with a sweet smile. "They haven't made a day long enough that I wouldn't wait for you."

Jackie couldn't help but laugh at her attitude. "Give these boys time," he retorted. "It's a three-game series." He turned serious again. "I don't care if they like me; I didn't come here to make friends. I don't even care if they respect me. I know who I am; I got enough respect for myself. But I do not want them to beat me."

Rachel took his hand and grasped it fiercely. "They are never going to beat you."

He sighed. "They're taking their best shot. I don't want you coming tomorrow. I don't want you to watch that, them beating me."

She just gripped his hand tighter. "Wherever you are, I am, too. Look at me, Jack." He did, though reluctantly. "I have to watch. So our hearts don't break. Plus, I already bought a scorecard." She held it up. His name was the only one filled in. "And I put your name on it. See? Jack Robinson."

He laughed and reached out for her other hand, twirling her around.

"I did good the day I met you," he told her.

Rachel grinned up at him. "Baby, you hit a home run."

The next day, the Phillies scored a run at the top of the first. Jackie stepped up to bat in the bottom half. And sure enough, Chapman was there to bait him.

"Hey, porch monkey!" he called. "Hey, Robinson! Hey, boy! You know why you're here?"

Motion from the Dodgers dugout caught Jackie's eye, and he turned in time to see Stanky launching himself forward. The fiery little guy headed straight for Chapman, who was still talking.

"You're here to draw those nigger dollars at the gate for

Rickey!" he was saying. Then he spotted Stanky coming toward him full tilt.

"Sit down," Jackie heard Stanky snarl as he closed the distance. "Sit down, or I'll sit you down."

"What's the problem, Stank?" Chapman asked.

"You're the problem, you disgrace!" Stanky replied, his voice carrying across the field. "What kind of man are you? You know he can't fight! Pick on someone who can fight!"

The two of them glared at each other for a minute. Finally, Chapman threw up his hands. "Okay, okay. Jesus." He returned to his dugout, and, suddenly free from distraction, Jackie hit a strong single.

Reiser was next, and he banged out a home run. Jackie jogged around the bases. When he reached the dugout, he sought out Stanky and plopped down next to him.

"Thanks," he told the second baseman.

Stanky shook his head. "For what? You're on my team. What am I supposed to do?" He rose to his feet and walked away, but not without muttering, "I gotta look in the mirror, too."

Jackie watched him go, and smiled. Today was turning out to be a pretty good day.

CHAPTER 12

ickey was sitting in his office, watching rain beat down against the windows, when Parrott rushed in. The younger man was soaking wet and clutching a newspaper he'd evidently cradled to keep from being destroyed. As he dropped into a chair, Rickey saw that it was the sports section of the *Herald Tribune*.

"The news isn't good, sir," Parrott warned.

Ricky sighed and leaned back in his chair. Things had been going reasonably well, lately. Dixie Walker continued to shun Jackie, but wasn't letting it interfere with his performance, and Rickey had just managed to trade the still-hostile Higbe to Pittsburgh for a bit of money and an Italian outfielder named Gionfriddo. Ah, well. He realized Parrott was waiting on him,

and smiled. "Nevertheless it must be accepted calmly, Harold. What is it?"

Parrott held up the newspaper so his boss could see the headline: "PLAYERS STRIKE." "'A National League players' strike,'" he read out loud, "'instigated by some of the Saint Louis Cardinals against the presence of Negro first baseman Jackie Robinson has been averted temporarily and perhaps permanently quashed.'" They both knew, though, that for it to have been started in the first place was a bad sign. And the Dodgers were playing the Cardinals next!

Rickey shook his head. "Madness! What are they thinking?"

Parrott didn't have any answers for him. The rain continued to beat down, but now it sounded more like something dark banging against the door, trying to find a way in.

Smith was waiting under an umbrella when the Cardinals pulled up to the Manhattan Hotel in their team bus. When the doors opened, the first person off was the manager, Eddie Dyer.

"Eddie," Smith called out, "what's all this talk about your Cardinals refusing to play?"

Dyer sneered at him. "We're here, aren't we? We didn't come to New York to go to Macy's."

Right behind Dyer was Big Joe Garagiola, but all he said

was "get lost" as he shoved past Smith. Stan Musial was a little more agreeable.

"This is big-league baseball, not English tea," he told Smith. "Couple a' guys might've popped off; it's hot air."

But Smith saw the glares from many of the other players, and knew it was a lot more than that.

Jackie sat at the training table, tending to his bat. The Dodgers had held practice despite the rain, and he didn't want his wood to warp. He was wiping it down with rubbing alcohol when Rickey came in and sat down beside him, holding a newspaper.

"National League president Frick says this is America, and baseball is America's game," Rickey declared, waving the rolled-up newspaper. "He says one citizen has as much right to play as another." A clap of thunder sounded outside, and Rickey winced as he continued, "Baseball will go on as planned once the rain stops."

Jackie eyed his bat rather than the man next to him. "Why are you doing this, Mr. Rickey?"

Rickey laughed and patted him on the shoulder. "Because my job is to win," he answered. "I have an obligation to Brooklyn to put the best team on the field that I can. Your presence on the roster increases our chances of winning."

Now Jackie did glance up. "If this is winning," he said, "I'd hate to see us on a losing streak." The thing was, the Dodgers had been winning more games than not. But he didn't believe for a second that was Rickey's only reason for bringing him onto the team.

Outside, the rain continued.

✕ ✕ ✕

Some of the other players were still in the locker room, changing into their street clothes, when Jackie gathered his things for a shower. He overheard Branca reading Reese something from the *New York Post*.

"Listen to this," Branca said. "'Right now Robinson is the loneliest man I have ever seen in sports.'" He threw the paper down. "Who's this guy to say Jackie's lonely?" he demanded. "He doesn't wear it on his sleeve. Man's got a fantastic game face. Take no prisoners. How does some reporter know how he feels?" Jackie thought he heard respect in his teammate's voice.

They quieted as Jackie walked past, but both Branca and Reese nodded to him. Walker, who stood beside them, did not. But that was nothing new.

"Lonely?" Branca commented after Jackie had passed. "I say it's the best game face in the world."

Just as he turned the water on, Jackie heard Walker reply: "So long as he showers lonely, he can have whatever face he wants."

The next day, the rain finally let up and the fields dried enough for them to play. Rachel was there in the stands, as always. And just a few rows in front of her, two men sat insulting her husband.

"Look, there he is!" the first one said, pointing to where Jackie stood at first. "Black as the ace of spades!"

His buddy shook his head. "You believe that? A genuine nigger in a Dodger uniform."

Rachel winced, but brightened a little when a Brooklyn fan leaned across the aisle and told them, "Shut up and go back to Saint Louis!"

Undeterred, the first Saint Louis fan exclaimed, "Hey, you got a nigger on your team!"

"So what?" the Dodgers fan replied. "He's better than anyone you got!"

"Wait till his cousin wants your job!" the second Saint Louis fan warned. "Don't you know nothing?"

The Dodgers fan waved that off. "Don't you?"

The first Saint Louis fan was staring out at the field again.

"He's a nigger!" he said again, as if he still couldn't believe it. "Hey, black boy!"

Rachel stared straight ahead, her back straight, and tried to ignore them. But it was hard to do through the tears threatening to spill from her eyes.

Meanwhile, the Dodgers had come up to bat and Jackie had stepped up to the plate.

"Watch this guy!" the Cardinals catcher, Garagiola, shouted down to third. "He can't hit! Especially the curve! He can only get on base bunting!" That was a particularly sharp insult to any solid hitter, no matter what color his skin, but Jackie ignored him and dug in. "Take your time, Robinson," Garagiola muttered to him. "You're digging your own grave."

Big Red Munger fired the pitch, and Jackie scooted back to avoid getting hit. There was a reason his bat had a thicker handle than most—the ball came at his chest and hands so often, he needed the extra width there to knock them away.

Trying to take his mind off that, he asked the catcher, "What's your average, Joe?" as he edged onto the plate again.

"It'd be a lot higher than yours, if I could run as fast as you can," Garagiola admitted.

Jackie laughed. "No matter how fast you run, you'll never hit as much as you weigh."

The catcher didn't like that much. "C'mon, Munger!" he

called to the pitcher. "Boy's got a hole in his bat!"

Munger threw inside again, but this time Jackie was ready for it. He fell back, and stroked a double into the gap between first and second. How was that for getting on base?

On the bus home that night, Rachel stared out the window. "Oh, Jack," she said sadly.

He put his arm around her. "What is it, Rae?"

"Nothing. It's just, sometimes when I sit up there with those loudmouths in the stands, I know you can hear them."

Jackie gave her a hug. "Don't worry. It's okay."

But she shook her head. "No, it's not okay. I can hear them, too."

Jackie looked at her, then moved his arm so he could take her hand in his. "I know. I'm sorry for that."

Rachel squeezed his hand back. "We're in this together. When they start in on you, you know what I do? I try to sit up straight."

He studied her. "Yeah?"

She nodded. "Straight as I can. I got it in my head that I can block it from you, some of it, if I sit up straight." She gave him a sad little smile. "Isn't that dumb?"

Jackie stroked her hand. "It worked. I didn't hear a thing."

She tried to smile for real, but tears rolled down her cheeks and she just couldn't manage it. Jackie leaned in and kissed her forehead.

"They're just ignorant," he told her.

Rachel gazed up at him. "If they knew you, they'd be ashamed." She wrapped her arms around him.

Jackie smiled down at her and held her close. "Hold on."

"I am holding on," she promised.

He smiled and kissed her again. "Long as we hold on, it'll be okay."

Rachel hoped he was right. But just in case, she planned to hold on as tight as she could.

CHAPTER 13

"You look lovely, Mrs. Robinson," Rickey told Rachel a few days later. They sat in the stands together watching Jackie at batting practice.

She smiled. "Thank you." She hadn't met the general manager often, but when she had she'd thought he seemed like a good, decent man. And she knew Jackie respected him a great deal.

"I don't know how you do it," Rickey continued. "Every day, from the first to the ninth. Myself? I could pay a hundred bucks for a suit and in twenty minutes I'd look like I fell out of bed. Even my shoes look rumpled."

They watched Jackie crack one high off the beer sign that loomed over the outfield.

“I used to think Jack was conceited,” Rachel offered out of nowhere, as her thoughts and memories spun around her.

Rickey glanced at her, his bushy eyebrows rising. “Is that so?”

She nodded. “It was the very first thing I noticed about him.”

“How did you two meet?” Rickey asked, leaning back in his seat. He sounded genuinely interested.

Rachel smiled. “I saw him at a UCLA football game. Even in uniform with a helmet on, his vanity was awful. It was the way he held his hands on his hips. I hated him!” Rickey laughed at that. “And on campus he always wore crisp white shirts and I’d think, *His skin is so dark, why would he do that?* Then I got to know him, his pride and confidence, and I realized he was showing off his color. I was wrong. He wasn’t conceited; he was proud. Always, of who and what he is. I’d never met another man like that.” She turned to study her companion. “What about you? How did you meet your wife?”

The smile he offered in return was sweeter than any she’d seen on him. Business and baseball were momentarily forgotten as Rickey told her the story. “I was trying to catch her in a race. She was the fastest girl in town. Beautiful legs. I finally caught up; we’ve been together ever since.”

Neither of them spoke for a moment. Below, Jackie nailed another fastball.

"I wanted to apologize to you," Rickey said finally, his voice serious again.

That surprised her. "For what?"

"Everything." Rickey gestured down toward Jackie. "I can't apologize to him. He and I both knew what we were getting into. But you, a newlywed, trying to begin a marriage under all this pressure?"

"Don't worry about me," Rachel assured him. "Or us. We know who we are." She hadn't been so sure of that at first, on that first trip down to Daytona Beach, but she was now.

"Your husband has humbled me," Rickey told her over the crack of Jackie hitting another ball. "When this all began I thought I was changing the world and that Jackie was my instrument. Can you imagine?" He shook his head. "I wish I could help him, but I'm just a spectator."

Rachel wanted to pat his hand, but she restrained herself and settled for telling him, "You help him plenty. Believe me."

"Is he able to get things off his chest?" Rickey asked then. "So he doesn't burn up?"

She smiled. "I have to let him have that silence at first, let him come to me. But he opens up eventually."

He nodded. "Good. It's too much to carry inside. Does he have any friends on the team?" He didn't miss the look she gave him. "They're spectators, too. They do admire him, though."

She looked out to where Reese and Stanky played catch. "Do you think so?"

"Even the worst of us recognizes courage," he promised her solemnly. "Moral courage especially. I have to think they see it. Jackie's a man on trial. He's responding with glory and grace. No one can take their eyes off him."

Rachel sighed. "He's had himself on trial since the day I met him. No man is harder on himself or gets to himself worse than Jack. But I hope his teammates know they're on trial, too." She thought about some of the things Jackie had told her, some of the things she'd seen. Some of his teammates treated him well enough, but others—they still couldn't get used to the way the world was changing. She wasn't sure they ever would.

Rickey was digesting her last statement, and now he nodded. "I suppose we all are. You're an astute woman, Mrs. Robinson."

That made her laugh. "I have to be, Mr. Rickey," she said with a smile. "I'm married to a man of destiny. I can't let him down."

He patted her hand in a friendly fashion, and there was a twinkle in his eye when he responded, "If I'd met you first, I wouldn't have looked so long for Jackie."

Rachel frowned. "How do you mean?"

"If he was good enough for you, he's certainly good enough for the rest of us."

Rachel ducked her head to acknowledge the compliment, and they sat there companionably watching her Jackie pound ball after ball out across the field.

The next day, Rickey had a far less pleasant conversation.

"Branch, it's Herb," Phillies general manager Herb Pennock said after Rickey had answered the phone.

"What can I do for you, Herb?" Rickey replied. He could tell from Pennock's tone that he hadn't called just to chat.

"How long have we known each other?" Pennock asked.

Rickey frowned. "Twenty years. Maybe more."

He heard the other man take a breath. "Then trust me when I say, Brooklyn's due here tomorrow, but you cannot bring that nigger down here with the rest of your team."

Rickey gritted his teeth at the insult but managed to stay civil. "And why's that, Herb?" he asked. "His name's Jackie Robinson, by the way."

"We're just not ready for this sort of thing in Philadelphia," Pennock told him bluntly. "I'm not sure we'll be able to take the field against your team if that boy is in uniform."

"Herbert," Rickey replied, "what your team does is your decision. But my team is coming to Philadelphia. With Robinson. If we have to claim the game as a forfeit, we will.

That's nine nothing, in case you forgot." A number like that would do a world of good for the Dodgers, actually, but Rickey didn't want to win that way, and he knew his team would feel the same.

Pennock was clearly getting worked up now. "Branch," he declared, "you've got a real bee in your bonnet about this thing and I, for one, would like to know what you're trying to prove."

Rickey didn't answer him directly. Instead, he asked, "Do you think God likes baseball? I do."

"What does that mean?" Pennock snapped.

Rickey leaned back in his chair and smiled, letting a little iron creep into his voice. "It means you're going to meet God one day, Herb, and when he inquires why Robinson wasn't on the field in Philadelphia and you answer because he was a Negro, it may not be a sufficient reply."

Then he hung up the phone. But he couldn't shake the feeling that things in Philadelphia were about to get mighty interesting. He hoped the team could handle it.

The trouble started when the team bus pulled up to the Benjamin Franklin Hotel. Parrott hopped off first. "Come on, fellas!" he called over his shoulder. "We have twenty minutes to check in and then get to Shibe! Chop-chop."

But just as the driver was opening the lower compartment so the players could grab their bags, the hotel manager came bustling out, followed by a pair of security guards.

"Out!" he shouted. "Get that bus out of here!"

"We're the Dodgers," Parrott told him quickly. "We have a reservation." He started to pull the confirmation letter from his folder, but the manager waved it off.

"Your team's not welcome," the man declared. "Not while you have ball club Negroes with you."

Everyone stopped and stared. "You mean Robinson can't stay here?" Parrott asked.

The manager glared at him. "I mean the entire team is refused!"

Now Parrott looked floored. "We've been staying here ten years."

"And you can stay away that long!" the manager snapped. Jackie hung his head, hating that his teammates now had to bear the brunt of harassment for him. At least he was used to this.

"Hold on, now," Shotton said as he climbed down off the bus. "Let's talk about this."

But the hotel manager jerked his thumb like an umpire. "Get out! Now, Grandpa!"

For the first time, Jackie saw Shotton lose his temper.

"Grandpa? Hey, hold on, you!" He made for the manager, but the security guards got between them.

Several of the other players turned, clearly intending to back their coach up—but they stopped short when Walker muttered, "Maybe Forty-Two's got enough friends in town, we can bunk up."

Jackie turned on the veteran player. "What's that supposed to mean?"

Walker shrugged, though a scowl covered his face. "Nothing. It's just, I know when you can't get into a hotel you got people's houses you can stay at." Somehow he made it sound like an accusation, like either Jackie felt he was too good to stay in hotels with the rest of them, or else he figured Jackie would take care of himself and leave the rest of the team to rot.

Jackie was tired of this. He closed the distance between them. "What do you want from me, Walker?" he asked.

If anything, the other man's scowl got fiercer. "An apology."

Jackie shook his head. "For what? Places like this?"

"For turning this season into a sideshow," Walker snapped. "I'm a ballplayer—I want to play ball!"

"So am I!" Jackie reminded him. "I'm here to win!"

Now Walker was in his face. "How are we gonna win sleeping on the bus?"

"Fellas—" Parrott tried to step in, but Jackie was too angry to listen to him.

"It might do you some good, the way you're swinging the bat lately."

"Watch your mouth!" Walker jabbed Jackie in the chest with a thick, blunt finger. Jackie batted his hand away.

"Watch your hand!" he shot back.

Walker lunged at him, and Jackie didn't back down an inch. But Reese, Stanky, and the others got between them, pulling them apart. Other players were dragging Shotton away from the hotel manager. Shotton was still shouting, "Grandpa? I'll show you Grandpa!"

Then Parrott loosed a shrill whistle, finally winning everyone's attention. "Fellas! Burt! Please!" he appealed. "Take the bus to the field! Worry about the game. I'll find another hotel."

They crowded back onto the bus, Branca and the others carefully keeping Jackie and Walker separated. Jackie wondered if his position with the team was getting better—or worse.

Parrott found Jackie and Smith later that night sitting in the visitors' locker room at Shibe Park, talking about what had happened earlier.

"Jackie, excuse me," Parrott started. He looked more nervous than usual. "Um, a request came in. The Phillies manager, Ben Chapman, he'd like his photo taken with you."

Jackie studied Parrott for a second, then made a show of sniffing the air around Parrott. "You been drinking, Harold?"

But apparently the team secretary was serious. "Mr. Rickey thinks it's a good idea," he explained. "He says it'll be in every sports page in the country. An example that'll show everyone even the most hardened man can change."

Jackie barked a laugh. "Chapman hasn't changed. He's just trying to take the heat off." He'd heard about the article that had been in the paper that day. It had compared the Phillies to a lynch mob.

Parrott just shrugged. "Mr. Rickey says it doesn't matter if he's changed. As long as it looks like he's changed. Chapman said he'd come down here. Or meet you in the runway."

Jackie's first instinct was to say no, that Chapman could go stuff himself. But Smith put a hand on his arm.

"See the ball come in slow," he reminded softly. "See the photo come in slower."

Jackie thought about that—and about what Rickey had told him, right at the start. He had to be the bigger man here. He had to show them all that he wasn't the one behaving badly. "Tell him I'll meet him on the field," he said finally. "Where everyone can see him."

Parrott smiled and nodded. "Perfect." He hurried out.

Sure enough, Jackie soon found himself standing with Chapman out by home plate. He even managed to keep his mouth shut as Chapman told the assembled reporters, "Jackie's been accepted in baseball, and the Philadelphia organization wishes him all the luck we can. I only hope in some small way our trial of fire helped him along."

It amazed Jackie that the Phillies coach could say that with a straight face. He hadn't realized Chapman was such a fine actor!

"How about a picture?" a photographer asked. He raised his camera. "Shake hands? Bury the hatchet?"

Jackie didn't really want to shake Chapman's hand, no matter how much he claimed he had changed. But Smith was nodding in the background, so he said, "You want a picture? Sure." Then he stepped over to the on-deck circle and grabbed a bat.

It was worth it just to see Chapman's eyes widen as he turned toward him, bat in hand.

"We'll hold the bat," Jackie told Chapman, too low for anyone else to hear. "That way we don't have to touch skin." The look of relief that crossed the coach's face proved how everything he'd just claimed had been a lie. He hadn't changed at all.

They each grabbed ahold of the bat, Chapman with both hands on the handle, Jackie with one hand on the barrel. He waited until the photographers were just about ready to start snapping before muttering, "Ben, I hope all your friends back home like the picture."

Chapman's jaw dropped, and his face went white. Jackie just smiled for the photo.

Sometimes, being the bigger man brought its own rewards.

CHAPTER 14

ackie squared off at home plate. The Pittsburgh Pirates pitcher, Fritz Ostermueller, flicked a glance at the catcher, Kluzt, then turned his steely glare on Jackie.

When he unleashed, the ball was aimed straight at Jackie's head.

There wasn't any time to duck. Jackie only managed to get his arms up to cover his face before the ball slammed into him. He went down in a heap.

Instantly, there was an uproar as Branca and several other Dodgers boiled out of their dugout and onto the field. The umpire intercepted them as best he could. Higbe, now in a

Pirate uniform, looked ready to cheer his new teammate for the hit.

"Ostermueller, you kraut!" Branca shouted at the pitcher. "You gotta bat, too! Don't you forget!"

"I'm ready, you wop!" Ostermueller replied with a sneer.

"It's gonna come right between your eyes! Like a kamikaze!" Branca warned hotly.

The Pirates pitcher gestured toward Jackie, who was shaking his head. "For him? He doesn't belong here!"

"You don't belong here," Branca retorted. "Go home to Goering and Shmelling!"

Ostermueller grinned, a big, nasty look. "Make me, you dago!"

Jackie sat up, one hand going to the big lump forming on his head. It hurt a whole lot, but he was okay.

"What can I do for you, Pee Wee?" Rickey asked as Pee Wee Reese entered his office in Brooklyn a few days later.

Reese shuffled his feet. "Well, Mr. Rickey, it's like this," he began. Rickey noticed that the shortstop was holding a folded paper in his hand. "The series in Cincinnati next week . . ." He trailed off.

"It's an important road trip," Rickey agreed. "We're only three games out of first."

Reese nodded. "Yes, sir. You know, I'm from Kentucky."

"Cincinnati's nearly a home game for you," Rickey commented. He already had a guess as to where this was going.

Reese stepped up to the desk and set the paper atop it. "I got this letter, sir. I guess some people aren't too happy about me playing with Robinson."

Rickey took the letter, unfolded it, and scanned its contents. "'Nigger lover,'" he read aloud. "'Watch yourself. We will get you, carpetbagger.'" He offered it back to Reese. "Typical stuff."

"It's not typical to me," Reese replied, taking the letter back. He looked surprised by Rickey's casual dismissal of it all.

Rickey sighed. "How many of these letters have you gotten, Pee Wee?"

"Just this," the shortstop replied. "Ain't that enough?"

Rickey studied Reese for a moment. Then he pushed back his chair and stepped over to a filing cabinet. Motioning for Reese to join him, Rickey pulled open a drawer and removed a stack of flattened letters, then another, then a third.

"What are those?" Reese asked quietly.

"I'll tell you what they aren't," Rickey answered. "They aren't letters from the Jackie Robinson fan club. Here—" He thrust a sheaf of them into Reese's hands.

Reese flipped through the stack of hate mail. "'Get out of baseball, or your baby boy will die,'" he read. "'Quit baseball or your nigger wife will be . . .'" His voice failed him, and he quickly flipped to another, his face pale. "'Get out of the game or be killed.'" The one after that shocked him so much he couldn't even read a word of it out loud. He looked up at Rickey, stunned. "Does Jackie know?" he asked finally.

Rickey tried to keep his voice calm. This wasn't Reese's fault, after all. "Of course he knows. So does the FBI. They're taking a threat in Cincinnati pretty seriously. So excuse me if I'm not too shocked at you being called a carpetbagger." He tried to smile. "You should be proud of it!"

"We'd just like to play ball, Mr. Rickey," Reese offered. "That's all we want to do."

Rickey nodded. "I understand. I bet Jackie just wants to play ball. I bet he wishes he wasn't leading the league in 'hit by pitch.' I bet he wishes people didn't want to kill him. But the world isn't simple anymore. I'm not sure it ever was. We just . . . baseball ignored it. Now we can't."

Reese nodded and set the letters down on the desk. "Yes, sir," he said quietly. "I gotta get to practice." He left without another word.

The Dodgers took the field at Crosley Stadium in Cincinnati on June 21. There were a lot more jeers and insults than Jackie

had heard in a while. He tried to ignore them, as usual.

Suddenly, Reese came jogging over to him.

"What's up?" Jackie asked. The abuse had gotten even louder, but now it wasn't just aimed at him.

"Carpetbagger!"

"Pee Wee, how can you play with that nigger?"

Reese looked sad and disappointed.

"They can say what they want," he told Jackie. "We're here to play baseball."

Jackie nodded. "Just a bunch of crackpots still fighting the Civil War."

Reese cracked a smile. "We'd a' won that son of a gun if the cornstalks had held out. We just ran out of ammunition."

Jackie laughed. He was impressed that his teammate could joke at a time like this. "Better luck next time, Pee Wee," he said, playing along.

Then Reese surprised Jackie by putting an arm over his shoulder. "Ain't gonna be a next time," he replied. "All we got is right now. This right here. Know what I mean?"

The gesture shocked the stands into silence, and after a second Reese smiled. "Thank you, Jackie." His tone was serious now.

Jackie looked at him, a teammate he'd always admired, but was just starting to know. "What're you thanking me for?"

"I've got family here from Louisville," Reese explained. He glanced up toward the stands. "Up there somewhere. I need 'em to know who I am."

Jackie didn't know what to say. He just nodded.

"Hey! Number one!" the umpire shouted at Reese. "You playing ball or socializing?"

Reese laughed and yelled back, "Playing ball, ump! Playing ball!" As he turned away, he told Jackie, "Maybe tomorrow we'll all wear forty-two. That way they won't be able to tell us apart."

Jackie watched his teammate walk away. He shook his head, then pounded his fist into his glove and got his head back in the game. Like Reese had said, they were here to play.

The next day, Jackie found himself sitting on the train playing gin rummy with Branca, Reese, and Smith. They were chatting and laughing over the cards, and he was amazed to realize that he was happy. He finally felt like he belonged, like he really was part of the team.

"You ever write about white guys in your paper?" Branca was teasing Smith. "I mean, if I threw a no-hitter and Jackie got a base hit, what would the headline be?"

"'Jackie Leads Dodgers to Victory. Again.'" Smith replied with a straight face. "Under that, 'White Italian Guy Does Okay.'"

They all laughed.

"I'd call your folks for ya, Ralph," Reese promised. "Tell 'em how you did."

Branca nodded. "No problem. It'll still make the *Post*."

"We are on some kind of winning streak, huh, boys?" Reese commented as he took a card.

"Hey, maybe forty of our last fifty," Branca agreed.

"Thirty-two and fifteen, actually," Smith corrected gently. "Since the fourth of July."

Branca grinned at him. "Math is why I throw a baseball for a living."

Reese discarded the card he'd just taken. "This next series against the Cardinals," he said aloud, "it's a big one."

Branca and Smith both nodded. Then they all turned to Jackie, who hadn't said a word.

"Whaddya say, Jackie?" Branca asked.

In response, Jackie laid his hand down on the little table. Then he looked at his two teammates and his part-time chauffeur. His friends.

"Gin," he told them.

CHAPTER 15

It was the top of the eleventh inning. The Dodgers and the Cardinals were tied at two. Jackie had knocked Stanky in with a double in the third, and Walker had done the same in the eighth. Hugh Casey was on the mound now, and Enos Slaughter had just stepped up to bat for Saint Louis. This was a big game—the Cardinals were still five games out, while the Dodgers had held first place since the end of June.

Casey threw a ball inside. Then another ball, low. But the third ball Slaughter knocked along the ground, straight toward Reese. The shortstop scooped it up and fired it over to Jackie, already on the bag. Slaughter was still fifteen feet out, but he didn't slow down. He just kept running, right across first base—

—and his cleated shoe came down hard on Jackie's right calf.

"Aahh!" Jackie went down, clutching his leg. Blood was already seeping through his sock.

Dodgers poured out of their dugout to protest, but the umpire waved them all back. It had looked like an accident, Slaughter not being able to slow down in time. Nobody believed that, though.

"Next batter, throw right at his head," Stanky urged Casey as they and Reese crowded around Jackie, checking to see if he was okay. "Clean his clock—"

But Jackie shook his head fiercely. "Just get him out. Understand? Game's too important."

As Casey nodded, Jackie reached up to Stanky and Reese. They pulled him to his feet. Jackie scanned the stands until he found Rachel, and gave her a wave to let her know he was all right. He'd worry about the leg later. Right now they had a game to win.

By the time Jackie got up to bat again, things weren't looking too good. The Cardinals had scored off them again, and now it was 3–2.

The first pitch almost took Jackie out at the knees. He

channeled his anger into his next swing and sent the ball hard up the middle, nearly taking the pitcher's head off. Served him right. "I don't care what happens," he muttered as he settled into his signature crouch at first. "I don't care what kind of play it is. When I get to second I'm gonna knock someone into center field."

Musial, the Cardinals' first baseman, glanced at the blood on Jackie's leg and nodded. "I don't blame you, man," he said sincerely. "You got every right." Which just reminded Jackie that every team had its decent members. Even this one.

Reiser bunted, and Jackie took off for second, sliding in. The Cardinal there, Schoendienst, saw him coming, saw the look on his face, and wisely got out of the way.

Jackie took a big lead off second as Walker stepped up to bat. He tensed, ready to run. Munger, the pitcher, glanced back, then at Walker—and then fired the ball to Marion, the shortstop, who was already on the move! Jackie leaped back toward second, but it was too late! He was out!

Jackie couldn't believe it. He was out! And that had been the third out for the Dodgers. The game was over. The Cardinals had won.

Reporters were all over him as he lay on the trainer's table after the game, getting his leg tended to.

“Did he spike you on purpose?” one of them asked.

“You saw the play,” Jackie answered. “I had my foot inside the bag. He was out by a mile. But he kept coming.”

“Slaughter said it was an accident,” another commented.

Jackie glared at him. “What are you asking me for, then?”

The reporter persisted. “Are you calling Slaughter a liar?”

Just then, Rickey showed up, a baseball in hand, and shooed the reporters away. “Get out,” he told them. “Let me talk to my first baseman. Go. He’s getting stitched up, for Pete’s sake!”

Rickey watched them go. “Sticking up for yourself is what you’d expect of any man,” he told Jackie. “Some find it galling to see it in a Negro.”

Jackie couldn’t look at him. “I’m sorry, Mr. Rickey,” he said softly.

“Sorry? Sorry for what?”

“I lost my cool out there,” Jackie admitted. “It probably cost us the game.”

Rickey chuckled. “I told you, Jackie, all the best base runners get caught sometimes.”

But Jackie shook his head. “I wasn’t thinking.”

Rickey pulled up a chair and sat down across from him. “Do you know what I saw this morning?” he asked. “I was passing a sandlot and a little white boy was up to bat. You know what he was doing?”

"Sitting on a fastball?" Jackie asked.

Rickey smiled. "He was pretending he was you. Wiping his hands on his pants, swinging with his arms outstretched like you do. A little white boy pretending he was a black man."

Jackie turned to face him finally. "Why are you doing this, Mr. Rickey?" he asked, as he had so many times before.

"We had victory over fascism in Germany," Rickey answered. "It's time for victory over racism at home."

But Jackie wasn't going to let it go this time. "Why are you doing this?" he asked again. "Come on now."

Rickey paused, looked away, and finally answered, his voice heavy. "I love this game. I love baseball. I've given my life to it. Forty-odd years ago, I was a player coach at Ohio Wesleyan University. We had a Negro catcher, best hitter on the team. Charley Thomas." He started slowly rubbing the baseball in his hands. "A fine young man. I saw him laid low. Broken because of the color of his skin, and I didn't do enough to help. I told myself I did, but I didn't. The game I loved had something unfair at the heart of it. I ignored it. But a time came when I could no longer do that." He looked up. "You let me love baseball again. Thank you."

Jackie nodded seriously. "You're welcome."

Blinking away tears, Rickey took refuge in his usual big pronouncements. "You're a force of nature, Jackie. You've

complicated everything but yourself. You're changing the world, and refusing to let it change you. I, for one, am in awe." Jackie could tell he meant it.

Jackie reached out and claimed the baseball. After a second, he declared, "I won't get picked off second base again. Not this year." That was a promise.

Rachel watched as Jackie packed.

"It's Pop's last long road trip of the year, little man," he told Jackie Junior softly. The baby slept on, undisturbed.

"Careful you don't wake him," Rachel warned.

Jackie smiled. "I know. I won't." He looked at her. "You okay?"

She shrugged. "I don't like seeing you leave, that's all."

"I'll be home in a week," he promised.

"Eleven days," she corrected. "That's a long time without you." He continued packing. Finally, she blurted out, "Try not to lunge at the plate."

Jackie looked up at her. "Seriously?"

She nodded, hugged herself. "That's why they're throwing the fastballs inside." He looked surprised, but she forced herself to continue. "Fight those inside fastballs off, foul them back. Sooner or later they won't be able to help but throw a curve."

He stepped over to her, smiling. "And what'll happen then?"

She pantomimed him hitting a home run, and the crowd going wild.

"We win enough of these next games," Jackie told her, "and we'll bring home the pennant." As if she didn't know that already!

But she mock-frowned and looked around their apartment. "Pennant? Where are we going to put a pennant? All these baby diapers hanging everywhere."

Jackie glanced about as well. "We got room right over there," he joked. "Between number one and number two."

"Win one if you have to," Rachel told him, "but bring yourself home. That'll be plenty."

He took her in his arms and kissed her. "Rae, you're in my heart."

"Promise me you'll come home," she said. "That you'll always come home."

He nodded. "I promise."

It was the bottom of the eighth and the Cardinals had two on and two outs. They'd cut the Dodgers' lead down to two, and Nippy Jones was up, with Musial on deck.

"Come on, Casey," Jackie hollered at the Dodgers' relief pitcher, "get him out! Pitch that ball!"

Casey threw, and Jones swung. *Crack!* The ball popped up, heading toward first but then arcing out of play. It was a foul. But Jackie saw a chance to end the inning right then. He took off after it, running hard right toward his own dugout. There! He flung himself into the air, catching the ball solidly—but as he came down, his left foot found nothing but air.

And then Branca was there, leaping forward from the dugout to tackle him back onto the field safely.

"He's got it!" Jackie heard the announcer shout. "And one of the Dodgers has him!"

Jackie sat in the locker room after the game. They'd done it, closed out the Cardinals and maintained their spot. Next was Cincinnati, for three games against the Reds. Most of the others were showering, and Branca was heading that way, a towel around his waist. But he stopped when he saw Jackie sitting there alone.

"Can I ask you something, Jackie?" the young pitcher said. "How come you never shower until everyone else is done?"

Jackie stared at him, wondering if he really didn't know, but Branca wouldn't let it drop.

"You shy or something?" he asked.

Jackie shrugged and looked away. "I don't want to make anyone uncomfortable."

Branca shook his head. "We're a team. On a hot streak. Half the wins on account of you. You're the bravest guy I ever saw. You're leading us and you're afraid to take a shower?" Jackie looked at him, and Branca smiled. "C'mon. Take a shower with me." Then he laughed. "Hey, I don't mean it like that."

All chatter stopped and everybody looked over as Branca entered the showers—followed by Jackie. Then everyone went back to talking and joking and getting clean. Jackie was surprised by how much that meant to him. But he did notice Dixie Walker leaving. *Who's the loneliest man on the team now?* Jackie wondered. He was pretty sure it wasn't him anymore.

Jackie settled himself at the plate. It was September 17. They were at Forbes Field, facing Pittsburgh again. They'd swept Cincinnati, all three games, and almost guaranteed themselves the pennant—if they could win today.

But it was Pittsburgh. And Ostermueller was pitching.

"You don't belong!" he shouted at Jackie, his face red. "You'll never belong!"

Jackie just waited for the pitch.

It was outside. Jackie didn't move. Ball one.

The second one was low and away. Ball two.

The third was outside as well. Ball three.

Was he just going to walk him? "Give me something I can hit!" he shouted at the mound. And he muttered to himself, "What are you afraid of?" Was Ostermueller really that worried about what Jackie could do? Jackie felt a surge of pride and power. Maybe he was.

The Pirates pitcher scowled at him. "You want it?" he hollered back. He tensed, wound up, and let fly.

Crack!

"Back, back, back," Jackie heard the announcer shout, "and oh, doctor! Robinson got his pitch!"

That ball was gone!

Jackie dropped the bat and started toward first. Then second. The Dodgers fans were going wild. Even the Pittsburgh fans were clapping. He felt a smile stretch across his face as he ran. He could almost see Rachel, watching him proudly. And Rickey, waiting to shake his hand. Jackie rounded third and headed toward home plate. All his teammates were waiting for him, and he laughed from sheer joy.

Finally, Jackie Robinson was home.

Dodgers
1946
HERE
FRIDAY
SAT.
SUN.
BALLS
OUTS
1 2 3 4 5 6 7 8 9 10 R P.
PLATE
BASES
1514 PITKIN AVE
WATCH FOR
DANNY
VIRGINIA

When Jackie Robinson participated in his first game as a Brooklyn Dodger on April 15, 1947, he became the first African-American athlete to play in Major League Baseball. He opened the door for other African-American athletes after him, and left behind an incredible legacy. Jackie was named Rookie of the Year in 1947 and was the first African-American to be voted the National League MVP in 1949. He was inducted into the Baseball Hall of Fame in 1962.

In 1972, the Dodgers retired his uniform number, 42. And in 1997, the league retired the number 42 across all teams, making Jackie Robinson the first player in any sport to have this honor. In 2004, the league instituted Jackie Robinson Day on the anniversary of his first game in the majors. April 15 is the only day that players are allowed and encouraged to sport the number 42 on their jerseys.